A WORD IN YOUR EAR

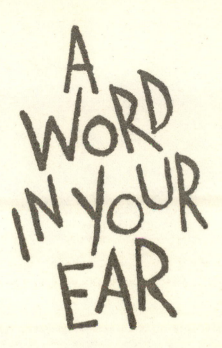

A collection of short stories from

TONY ROSS

ANDERSEN PRESS

First published in 2014 by
Andersen Press Limited
20 Vauxhall Bridge Road
London SW1V 2SA
www.andersenpress.co.uk

2 4 6 8 10 9 7 5 3 1

British Library Cataloguing in Publication Data available.

ISBN 978 1 78344 050 4

Printed and bound in Great Britain by
CPI Group (UK) Ltd, Croydon CR0 4YY

To Klaus, but that's another story.

Contents

Introduction   1

Art   3

Enemy   20

Escape   33

Friends   47

Garden   58

Heaven   71

Home   81

Olé   93

Promise   106

Raggedy   117

Schooled   130

Smile   144

Ted   158

Putting the record straight . . .   173

Introduction

I like autobiographies. I like to know about people. But the trouble with autobiographies is that writers tend to hold back the best parts; hold back all their darkest secrets.

So when I sat down one day to write my autobiography, I wanted to write about all the best parts of my life *and* about my darkest secrets. And as I started to write, I realised that a lot of my greatest and scariest memories had only *nearly* happened to me.

You see, every time I started writing about a particular time in my life, my imagination took over. When I was younger, for instance, I spent some time in Spain and met bullfighters like those in my story 'Olé'. Although the characters in this story are made up, I wanted to capture that moment in time, and tell a story about the lives of the young matadors.

And my story 'Escape' is based on my visit to 'the plague village' Eyam – I found myself starting to write a haunting tale about what it might have been like to live there during the time of the Great Plague.

So this is an autobiography with a twist. It's a collection of stories about things that *have* happened, have *nearly* happened, and things I imagined *could* have happened to me or to others. There is truth in all my stories, but they are not all true.

You have been warned, though – these are my darkest secrets . . .

ART

When Mum and I moved from London to Cornwall I didn't like the idea at all. For a start there were no good bands down there, or half-decent football teams.

'Chill!' said Mum. 'They do have electricity. You can watch the Gunners on TV. They're on all the time.'

'I can't hang out on TV, can I?' I sniffed.

'You'll have other things to do. The beaches are beautiful,' said Mum, searching for encouraging signs in my eyes.

'Hip hip hooray!' I muttered. 'I'll be able to take up collecting seashells. If any of my friends ever get on their camels to visit me down here, think of the sand castles we'll be able to build. Roll on summer.'

I decided to sulk for a bit to see if any bribes came up. They didn't.

'Now don't you give me a hard time,' sighed Mum. 'I can't afford to live in London any more, not since Dad left, and you *know* I have a job offer down there.' Mum's old friend, Natalie, had moved down to Cornwall three years ago and opened a hairdressing salon. Mum is a great stylist and Nat had promised her a job if she was prepared to move. '*Give it a year or so and there will be a partnership in it for you*,' Natalie had said.

So I guessed I'd better get used to it.

After what felt like the longest journey ever, we arrived in Cornwall at our new home – 'Turk's Head Cottage', which stood atop a cliff, just outside town. It was very old, painted white inside and out, and the walls inside were rough, with old beams which had been salvaged from a bygone sailing ship. Although I didn't want Mum to know it at the time, I thought the cottage was beautiful. Trouble was, it wasn't finished yet; a new kitchen was being put in, and the electrics needed completely re-doing. Mum planned to do a lot of redecorating herself too, and I was roped in to help with stripping old paper off the walls and general painting and tidying up.

Mum was quite excited about the new kitchen that was being fitted, but I rather liked the scruffy old one – it was a bit homemade, but it was part of the cottage and it suited our things. We didn't have much furniture with us when we moved from London, but we soon discovered that our new neighbours found it easier to give us stuff they no longer wanted than to go to the tip with it.

Until the cottage was ready, we had a tiny caravan in the garden, where Mum slept, and I spent the night in the cottage on my own, since one of the bedrooms had been dusted and was liveable in. At least I could get some sleep there – Mum snores a bit (she swears she doesn't, but she does), so I'd never have slept a wink crammed in with her in that tiny caravan.

The little room was at the front, overlooking the garden. It was quite small with dirty greyish-white walls that would, one day soon, be a sparkling *whitish*-white. The sloping ceilings were fitted to the inside of the roof, so the room went up to a point above me.

As the summer wore on I began to feel happier about being in Cornwall. I painted the beautiful scenery every morning – it looked different every day – and it became normal for me to go around barefoot, even into the village. My skin was beginning to turn a golden brown and I was sure my hair was more blond too.

I made a couple of friends, Tim and Alice, who had lived in the village their whole lives and were teaching me to surf – beaches do have their uses – and over the summer holidays I mixed learning to be a beach bum with helping Mum sort out the house. There was always lots to do, and at the end of these busy days we had our evening meal in the caravan and watched a bit of TV. Then off I would go to the cottage to bed.

My strange experience began at the end of August, when

we'd been living in Cornwall for a month. Mum and I had started to clear the garden, or rather clear our bit of heathland to make it look like a garden. This land was full of huge grey boulders and, as we couldn't shift them, Mum said they could stay and be garden features. They made useful seats with the cultivated bits around them. Anyway, what work we did was *backbreaking*, so we both needed a seat at times!

One night, we scoffed sandwiches and then headed for bed. As was always the way, as soon as I lay down I didn't feel tired any more, so I decided to read some more of my favourite series of books, *Adrian Mole* – I loved those books so much that I almost wanted to live in Leicester, where they're set. Reading in the cottage wasn't easy; my camp bed had no back, so I had to lie on one elbow, and the electrics weren't on yet, so I was reading by torchlight. On that particular night I felt very content. The air was warm and smelled of flowers and the sea, and the full moon made the landscape outside the window a wonderful picture of black and silver.

I stopped reading and looked towards the window. Then something made me get up and look out at the night. In the distance the sea glinted in the moonlight. But I looked down into the garden.

A figure was sitting on one of our 'garden features'. *Figure* was the wrong word; *apparition* is better. It was a man dressed in a short jacket, white trousers and sea boots. He wore a dark peaked cap, and his head was bowed. I watched, fascinated, my heart beating wildly, and I held my breath, lest the noise of my breathing gave me away. I was frightened then, but not as much as you might think.

I could make out the detail of the man because he was bathed in a gentle, grey light. My heart started to thump faster as the man began to move. Slowly, he lifted his head until our eyes met, and *now* a chill of fear washed over me, for the man's face was horrible.

His body was sturdy, powerful even, but his face was only a skull, with skin stretched tightly over it. Wispy silver hair hung down from his cap, with strands from his chin where a beard would have been on a living man.

The awful figure stood up and began to rise gently into the air, our eyes staying locked until his face was level with mine.

Frozen in his stare, I thanked my lucky stars that the window was closed. Then suddenly his colourless lips cracked apart, revealing white uneven teeth. He *smiled*. But his *smile* could so easily have been the snarl of a rabid dog . . .

Slowly the *thing* raised his arm and pointed. For one hideous minute I thought he was pointing at *me*, but he wasn't; he was pointing at the wall behind me.

I felt as if I had forgotten how to breathe and, as I stared out through the window at that face, it slowly began to disappear. The grey light was fading and with it the man, until only the cliffs and the beautiful sea remained.

I stood at the window for I don't know how long. I went back to bed, but all night my thoughts tumbled about in my head until the sun began to lighten the sky. Had I seen a ghost? Of course not; I didn't believe in ghosts. But then, just because I didn't believe in them, that didn't mean they didn't believe in me, did it?

As the new day brightened my room, I dozed off and snatched a few hours uneasy sleep. When I woke I scrambled into jeans and a T-shirt and rushed down to the caravan for breakfast to tell Mum about my experience.

'You could have been dreaming,' she said, fussing about with toast and boiled eggs.

Mums always say things like that – but you *know* if something's real, and what I had seen had *been* real. Mum wasn't really listening anyway; she had an idea that we should keep hens and she kept asking me if *I* thought it was a good idea. Soon, even I began to think about hens, real hens, and not about ghosts, that weren't real.

Perhaps what I thought I saw last night never happened? I told myself. *Maybe Mum's right and it* was *just a dream?*

•

After breakfast I went to the town and, on the way, stopped in on one of the oldest ladies living round there, Mrs Fitt. She was really kind to me and Mum, and baked amazing cakes for us. I sometimes got her shopping for her, or helped her out in the garden.

Mrs Fitt was tidying up a flowerbed in her garden, and after I'd said, 'No, thank you,' to another cup of tea and another breakfast, I told her about the night before. The old lady looked startled for a moment, and then flopped down on her garden bench.

'Oh, dearie,' she chuckled, 'you have seen Captain Vasey. He used to live at Turk's Head Cottage over a hundred years back. He sailed a clipper ship, the *Rowena*, as went down on the rocks along the coast. All hands were lost, including the captain. From time to time, he comes back to his old home, just to see who's living there now, we think.' She looked at my startled face and added, 'Don't worry, dearie, he will not come again. You'll not see him no more. Everyone who's seen him says that he just appears and points at the new owner of the cottage, as if he's sizing them up. He's only visited each person once, though.'

'So, other people have seen him?' I asked. 'Not just me?'

Mrs Fitt crinkled her nose. 'Course they have, dearie.

Old Vasey's a part of this village. Never seen 'im meself, though,' she finished sadly.

That night I felt easier about sleeping alone in the cottage, now knowing that the ghost had visited once and so would not come again until he had someone new to look at.

Mum had remembered my 'dream'. 'You can sleep here tonight if you like,' she smiled, when we were having our tea in the caravan.

'It's OK, Mum,' I replied. 'I'll be fine in the cottage.'

I decided not to read and fell asleep at once, but I awoke to a tapping at my window, and with a beating heart I pulled the duvet down below my eyes and peeped across.

Captain Vasey was there again, his bony fingers scratching at my window. I looked more carefully this time and noticed that his clothes were soaking wet – that matched the story Mrs Fitt had told me.

When he caught my gaze, his tight skin was pulled back over his skull in that same wolf-like grin, and he pointed at the wall again, just like he had the night before.

I was more disturbed this time. *Why has this thing visited me twice?* I felt threatened, haunted. Slowly I climbed out of bed and crept out onto the landing, away

from the terrifying apparition, but to my horror Captain
Vasey was there, blocking the stairs! Smiling, he held out
his bony arms towards me and I rushed back into my
room, but now the ghost was outside the window again,
pointing.

Then, suddenly, just as before, the image began to
fade until it was lost in the early dawn.

I think that Mum half-believed my story the next morning. She didn't believe in ghosts, but then she had always
trusted me to tell the truth, so she was in a hard place.
After breakfast, we both went back into the cottage and
up to the small bedroom.

We'd stripped the wallpaper in there the day before,
as we were planning to paint it later in the week. I
showed Mum the place on the wall where the ghost
had pointed to, and we noticed that in the middle of the
rough stone there was an outline of a square of plaster.

'I didn't spot that yesterday,' said Mum. She tapped
the area; it sounded hollow, so we chipped away at the
plaster, which fell away easily, revealing a faded green
wooden cupboard door.

Behind the door was a small space, filled with a
bulky bundle of thick papers. Excitedly we took them
back to the caravan and laid them out on the little table.
They were paintings of ships, coves and harbours: not

like photographs, but carefully finished in the most extraordinary and vivid colours. One was of the clipper ship *Rowena* entering the harbour. They were wonderful paintings, each one signed 'Vasey'.

We put them out against the wall and admired each one in turn. We couldn't believe we'd found this treasure trove of beautiful old artwork, and we just kept looking at each other and laughing like two little kids.

'Mum,' I said quietly, 'these are all by Captain Vasey, the ghost, aren't they? I think he meant for me to find them, maybe because I love painting this seascape too. What do you think we should do with them?'

Mum didn't say anything for ages; she was just as surprised as me. And she knew now that I'd been telling the truth about the ghost.

'I think he'd want people to see them, don't you?' I added.

'Yes,' said Mum. 'I think you must be right.' Then she looked at me as if she was slightly awed by me; she'd never looked at me like that before.

Mum and I took the pictures to an art gallery in the nearest town, where the man who ran it became so excited that he offered us a thousand pounds for them on the spot.

Mum thought that was fantastic, but I said we

would think about it and let him know. I didn't know how much they were worth, but they seemed very special to me and I wasn't ready to let go of them just yet.

'Fifteen hundred!' said the man.

'We'll be in touch!' I said.

When we got outside the gallery, Mum turned on me. 'Fifteen hundred quid! You turned down fifteen hundred quid! Are you *nuts*?'

'I think they are more special than fifteen hundred quid,' I said.

Back at home we looked at the pictures again; they really were beautiful.

'Tell you what,' said Mum. 'Terence, Nat's ex-husband, runs a gallery in London, near Bond Street. He only shows the very best artists' work. Let's see what he says.'

I didn't see Captain Vasey that night or the one after, but I wondered if he was happy now that I'd found the paintings. I felt too that, as he'd chosen me to find the paintings, I had to make sure that I did with them what he would have wanted – it wasn't as if I knew much about him, but I was a bit of an artist myself, and I knew that if I could have my work shown anywhere, I'd definitely like it to be in a smart gallery in London. I'd know that my art was worth something then.

•

A few days later, we took the train to London. When we got off at Paddington, I breathed in London – it felt good to see and smell the city again.

We got to Terence's gallery and Captain Vasey's paintings were laid out. Terence could not praise them enough; in fact, he called them 'important'. And after a posh lunch, he said that he would love to put on an exhibition of them, to sell them on our behalf, and we could leave all the details to him. I was so pleased; it almost was as though Terence were putting on an exhibition of my work, it felt so personal somehow.

When we got back to Cornwall I couldn't wait to find out more about Captain Vasey, so I went to the local library and did some research, which I sent on to Terence.

Captain Vasey was born in Liverpool and went to sea as a boy, in the Royal Navy. After many adventures, he learned his trade as a seaman, and with his prize money he bought a little trading sloop and made his fortune. His next ship was the Rowena, *a clipper, which he sailed all the way to China and back.*

By that time, Captain Vasey had bought Turk's Head Cottage in Cornwall, and on his few days ashore he taught himself to paint pictures. He painted what he knew, the ships and the ports of his lifetime. His love of the sea changed to a love of painting, so he intended to retire to his cottage, forsaking the sea, and live the life of an artist. But the sea was a jealous mistress and took the Rowena *and everyone aboard in the dreadful storm of 1859, cheating Vasey of his dream of finding fame as an artist.*

In time, we received an invitation to the private view of an exhibition in London, entitled 'Vasey, a Lifetime at Sea'. Terence had produced a beautiful catalogue, with pictures of some of the paintings, and notes including my research on Captain Vasey.

When we got there, the gallery was crowded and there were lots of reporters. Each of the pictures had been beautifully mounted and framed; they looked very professional up there on the gallery walls. There were little red spots on most of the frames, and when I asked Terence what they were for, he said those pictures had already been sold.

As I sipped my orange juice, things around me suddenly began to change. The babble of voices seemed muffled, I felt a sudden chill in the air, and then everyone in the gallery faded away so that I felt like I was the only one in the room.

Just me and one other – a strongly built man I hadn't noticed before stood with his back to me. He was wearing sea boots and a peaked cap and I held my breath as the man slowly turned to look at me. The skull-like face I was preparing myself for had changed, however; instead, a strong, sun-weathered face, with warm brown eyes and a full, black beard, looked at me.

The face was different, but it was still my ghost. Still Captain Vasey. The captain continued to stare at me for a moment, and then his face broke into a happy smile. Although he was surrounded by people, I was the only one who seemed to know he was there – he seemed real and solid, but standing amongst an audience of ghosts.

Slowly he began to fade, and when he was gone the room came to life again and the bustling crowds in the gallery went on as if the captain had never appeared.

'Did you see him, Mum?' I asked excitedly.

'See who?'

Back at Turk's Head Cottage I hung a picture, signed 'Vasey', over the fireplace. It was of his clipper ship, the *Rowena*, entering our local harbour.

'Gosh,' said Mum, 'where did *that* come from? It's worth quite a lot of money now, I think!'

'I kept it back,' I said, 'in case Captain Vasey ever returns. He may like to see it hanging in his old home.'

A month later, a huge cheque came from the gallery in

London. Mum danced around the garden waving it in the air. It was for a *lot* more than the £1500 the local gallery had offered us.

'We can afford London again, if you want?' she said.

'No, I think I would rather stay here,' I answered, 'for ever!'

We lived at Turk's Head Cottage for years after that, and although I never saw Captain Vasey again, I knew he was always there . . .

A note about *Art*

The funny thing about ghosts is: it is possible to see a ghost in the dark of night, and yet the next day to just *know* that they don't exist. I have seen several, and I still don't believe in them.

This story is based on an experience I once had. I was helping a friend repair an old cottage, near to the coast. He slept in a caravan and I slept in the cottage. That night I looked out of my window and saw a strange ghostly figure. My friend had seen it too, as had many people in the village. The ghost was not threatening or scary, but somehow I *was* scared. I've never forgotten it, and often wondered who it was. Some of the local people claimed to know – some of them thought it was an old mistress of the house, who always appeared once to cast an eye over the new occupants.

Everyone agreed that once you had seen it, you would never see it again. And – do you know? – not one of those people believed in ghosts.

ENEMY

One of the worst things about war, or *the war* as we called the Second World War, was that my gran would get very nervous whenever I went out by myself. That may not have *all* been the war's fault; that may have been because I was only six years old at the time.

Gran and Kenny both told me how dangerous the war was – Gran heard all about it on the wireless, and Kenny knew all about it because he was an evacuee from London, where the Germans had aimed bombs at him. Luckily Kenny had been too quick for them, and he now lived with us in the country.

Gran was not going to be caught out by the Germans, either, so she wore her tin hat all the time, except for church – she even wore it in bed, just in case.

Everyone talked about the war all the time and my friends and I would wave at the Spitfires as they growled overhead. At first, I didn't realise these planes were even part of the war – they just seemed to be having fun in the air. Later, though, I found out that lots of them had been shot down overseas, and their pilots killed, or taken prisoner. 'Prisoners of war', they were called, and some of them were locked up in Germany.

But it wasn't just British pilots who were taken prisoner; there were also German prisoners of war, and we had some of them in our village. I thought they were probably the pilots of German Spitfires that had been shot down by us.

Our German prisoners of war lived on a piece of waste ground – the Croft – in an air-raid shelter. They didn't wear chains or anything like that; they just wore grey suits with big yellow patches sewn on the backs and legs. I thought that the patches were where their suits had been mended, but Kenny told me they were targets to shoot at, in case the prisoners ran away.

But the prisoners didn't seem to want to run away. I supposed that was because, firstly, there was nowhere to run to; and, secondly, the buses only ran twice a day, so it would be easy to miss them. And you couldn't get anywhere near us without getting on a bus – mostly we were surrounded by lots of country. Sometimes, a soldier with a gun came to check on the prisoners, and he brought them letters and other things too; men in macs also visited regularly to check up on how well the prisoners were doing. I knew all this because I spied on them sometimes.

Their air-raid shelter was quite a long way from the

road and the prisoners were set to work building a track from the road to the back of Gittins' farm. They always seemed quite happy to do it, but they also spent a lot of their time just lying in the sun. When one of the soldiers with guns came near, they jumped up and grabbed their shovels; when he left them alone, they just lay down again. Mr Gittins said that he was not fussed about a road, anyway.

As the days grew longer, Gran said that it would be OK for me to go out and play by myself. I'd had to sneak out up till this moment so I was pretty happy.

'Be back in time for tea,' she said, 'and don't go near the Germans!'

'How can I go near the Germans?' I said. 'Germany is *miles* away.'

Gran hit out at me, but missed. She always missed. 'You know what I mean, you cheeky monkey,' she snapped. 'The Germans who live on the Croft, the prisoners building the road. I mean it! They are *bad*, they are the *enemy*. If they catch you, they will eat you!'

I couldn't wait to go and spy on the Germans again, but I didn't want to go alone. The sun was warm, so I went round to my friend Terry's house. He wasn't there, so I strayed towards the Croft, making sure not to let the Germans see me, in case they were feeling hungry.

The Croft was a good place. People threw things away there – Terry found a pram wheel once, and he only needed three more to start building a pram. I searched happily as the afternoon burned on, not noticing how close I was getting to the prisoners' shelter. Suddenly there they were – four men, talking in another language and laughing. I tried to duck down, but they had seen me. They put down their plates of beans and beckoned me over.

'Not on your nelly! You're not having *me* with your beans.' I turned and fled. I wasn't frightened, you understand; it was just that I thought it was time for tea.

Next day, I went back to the Croft. Child-eating Germans were easily the most interesting things around. Also, they couldn't have been *that* hungry – they had lots of beans and bread and cups of something. I sat down in the long grass close to the shelter and thought about it.

They can't want to eat me, I don't taste nice at all. I know that because when that scab came off my knee I ate that and it didn't taste of much, I reasoned.

Cautiously I stood up. I spotted two of the Germans messing about outside their shelter and they noticed me and waved. The taller of the men took something out of his pocket, and waved it towards me. I couldn't see what it was so I edged forward.

'Hey, boy,' he called. 'Chocolate!'

Gran had told me about chocolate, how you could get it before the war and how wonderful it was. I reached out and took the sweet and nibbled a bit – Gran was right, it was delicious!

Then the other two Germans came out of the shelter, and when they saw me they smiled. 'Hello,' said one, who was quite fat. 'My name is Friedrich.'

'And I am Günter,' said the other. 'What are you called?'

As the fat one looked hungry, I dashed off, scrambling through ferns and brambles. When I got home, I found Kenny painting his bike brown and green like a Spitfire. I told him all about the chocolate and how good it had tasted.

Kenny stood up. 'Look out, Toad,' he grinned. (That's what he called me as a nickname – 'Toad'.) 'They're fattening you up.'

I hadn't thought of that. 'I don't think so,' I said. 'They're friendly, and they speak English.'

'Everybody speaks English,' said Kenny. 'That doesn't mean anything.'

'They speak German too,' I replied.

'That shows how cunning they are. That shows that they *are* going to eat you.'

I supposed Kenny must've been right – he was older

than me and knew more things. On the other hand, the prisoners had given me chocolate and were very friendly.

Terry called in that evening, and I asked him whether or not Germans eat children.

'Course they do,' said Terry. 'Usually boiled with sprouts. They have black puddings and custard afterwards, my mum says.'

Not only that, but he wouldn't come and spy on them with me.

I didn't go back to the Croft for some days, but after a while I couldn't resist it. After all, the German prisoners had seemed so nice and I was curious about them. Somehow, I couldn't really feel frightened of them.

Quite soon I found myself visiting the air-raid shelter every day, and quickly felt at home there. Three of the prisoners spoke English well, while the other – Willi – could only say 'Hello', 'Goodbye' and 'Thank you'. He smiled in English though. They had some interesting food, things I had never tasted before, and they shared everything with me. They had beer too, and one day Klaus let me try some. He took a thimble out of his sewing kit, filled it with beer and held it out to me. I sipped it, but it only tasted like water, rather smelly water. I spat it out, and they all laughed.

The only time we mentioned the war was when the

prisoners told me what they wanted to do if they ever went home.

Friedrich was a baker, as were his father and grandfather; he longed to go back to that life again.

Günter played the cello and he dreamed of being in a great orchestra. 'If I can't do that,' he said sadly, 'maybe I teach school.'

'Don't do *that*,' I pleaded. 'You are too nice. Teachers are mouldy.'

Everybody laughed.

Klaus said that he was a printer and would like to do that again.

'What does Willi want to do?' I asked.

Klaus said something to Willi in German and Willi smiled and replied in German. Then he said, 'Please?'

Klaus looked at me and said, 'Willi wants to be a chef. And he says, what do *you* want to be, when you are bigger?'

'I want to be a German,' I said, and everybody laughed again.

One day I took a piece of chocolate home for Kenny.

'Not blooming likely!' he said. 'It's probably poisoned.' Then he threw it to the dog, who decided to take the risk. The dog is still OK.

I told Kenny all about my new friends. I didn't think

Gran could hear, sitting over by the window, reading her *Woman's Weekly* by the last light of the day. But then, suddenly, she straightened her tin hat and marched over to me. She seemed very angry.

'What did I tell you about Germans?' she barked. 'They are *bad*, *bad*, *bad*.' She went on and on about the enemy, and told me the many ways I could be cooked and eaten, if I ever went near the Croft again. Finally she pointed to a photograph hanging on the wall. 'What's more,' she whispered, as if there were spies about, 'if you talk to the enemy again, Mr Churchill will *never* forgive you.'

She stared at me and frowned. Then, looking again at Mr Churchill, she stood to attention and tipped her tin hat over her eyes.

'Think on!' she said.

I thought on, and for days I didn't go near the Croft. It rained a lot around that time and so the grass would have been dripping anyway.

But everything ends, and as the rain did, I gradually forgot about Mr Churchill's disapproval. The days became sunnier and I began to miss visiting the German prisoners of war. One day, my wanderings took me back up onto the Croft. I suppose I just wanted to see if the prisoners were still there. Apart from Mr Churchill, I didn't want to upset Gran.

I crept closer to the shelter and, to my dismay, there was nobody sitting on the grass outside. I tiptoed over to the door and listened. All I could hear was my heart beating, but then, at last, I heard voices inside, German voices.

Happily I rushed into the shelter, but stopped in my tracks because as I came through the door, the four men jumped up, looking surprised and guilty.

And it was all true . . . they *were* going to cook me! They had bits of wood for the fire, and they all had long, sharp knives to kill me with.

As Willi and Klaus tried to hide the wood and the knives in their bedding, Günter started towards me.

'Boy!' he said.

I stumbled back into the daylight, and ran and ran and ran.

I was crying when I got home.

I told Gran everything, and she let me wear her tin hat for a while, to calm me down.

August passed, and soon it was time to go to school again. My close escape from being eaten faded into a distant memory, but I just had to have one last look at the enemy so, on the last afternoon of my holiday, I ventured again onto the Croft.

Keeping low, I crept through the bushes and peeped

at the air-raid shelter. The four men were outside, eating and laughing. I sneaked closer, to try and catch their words. Closer and closer; I couldn't help it.

Suddenly Willi looked in my direction and pointed. The men stood up and I panicked and ran, jumping through grass and the brambles that tore at my legs.

Then, with a yelp, I went flying. I had tripped over an old pram wheel, lying hidden in the grass. I hit the ground, winded, and looking up, I saw the Germans standing over me.

Willi picked me up and carried me back to the shelter, where I was laid on a bunk. Klaus dabbed the blood from my scratched legs, as the others fished about for chocolate. Finally Klaus sat me up and offered me chocolate, but I was too frightened to take it.

'Come on, boy,' he said, 'we have something else for you.'

As I looked wildly around for the cooking pot and the spices they would have to use to make me taste nice, Günter fumbled in the bedding and pulled something out, something wrapped in newspaper.

I undid the paper, and inside there was a sort of wooden paddle, like a ping-pong bat. Two beautifully carved hens were on the top, and their necks and tails moved when you moved the bat. There was a wooden ball hanging underneath on a string, and as it went to and fro, the hens looked as if they were pecking food. I held the toy, watching the wooden beaks clacking on the bat.

'We made it for you,' smiled Günter. 'It took a long time. Once, you came in and saw us fixing it. We tried to hide it, but you ran away so it was OK.'

I looked up at the four kind faces of my friends and whispered, 'Thank you.'

I knew then that they definitely would never eat me.

A note about *Enemy*

This story is based on my memories of four German prisoners of war that were billeted near my home and were very kind to me. They did indeed give me a wooden toy just like the one in this story.

I can't remember their names or anything like that, but then the best stories have made-up bits, don't they? I remember their clothes and their faces, and their kindness. The wooden hen toy was lost years ago, but I loved it until I lost it. I wonder if someone has it now?

Those German prisoners of war were so nice, and some of the English people around me were so nasty (like some of my teachers!) that I wondered why we were the 'goodies' and they were the 'enemy'. This experience made me think, for the first time, what on earth was the sense of war?

On the other hand, maybe I understood at that young age that there really is no sense in war.

ESCAPE

Robert Atherton settled back in his chair and gazed at the logs spitting on the hearth. He felt tired and every bone in his body ached. The long journey from London to Derbyshire had taken its toll, and Robert looked forward to stretching his legs on the moors, but that would have to wait until tomorrow, when the feeling of life came back to his exhausted body.

It was late August, 1665. Robert had had as much of London as any man could, and his wool exporting business was slowing down due to the plague – a plague horribly like the medieval Black Death that had killed so many, and still known as 'a black death' due to the livid black spots that appeared on the bodies of those shortly to die.

The king had left London for Oxford long ago, and others, rich enough to leave, were leaving too. Recently, several of Robert's friends in Houndsditch had boarded up their premises and sought the cleaner air in the country for their families. Robert himself was a bachelor and had no ties to keep him in or near the city. Having grown up in Derbyshire, he had maintained a house there, both as a place to relax and to keep sheep for his wool business, so he'd sent his belongings ahead and stayed in London only long enough to tie up his business affairs and close his house.

He was very relieved to have escaped the city – last week alone some six thousand souls there were said to have died from the plague. But as he gazed into the fire he relived the strange events of his journey . . .

He had left London early, his horse was young and he'd made good time. By early evening he was well clear of Hertford but then the weather had turned. Black clouds brought an early twilight, and the driving rain made it difficult to see the road ahead. Robert pulled his sodden cloak around him and peered through the water cascading from his hat as his horse floundered on, stumbling through the mud. Eventually he dismounted to give her some relief.

But it was hopeless to travel on. The mud made it impossible even to tell if he was on road or field, so he had no way to judge what part of the county he might be in. It seemed that the best thing to do was to seek some shelter for the night and carry on in the morning.

But *where*? Robert had left the last village behind some hours ago, and now there seemed nothing but bleakness around him. Then, as darkness settled, he thought he saw a glimmer of light some way off and he headed as fast as he could in that direction.

A large, stone farmhouse slowly came into view, nestling in a fold in the landscape. The downstairs windows were lit with a friendly glow, and the whole place had an air of welcome. Relieved to have found shelter, Robert made his way to the door, which was shrouded in darkness, and banged on it. His horse was shivering now, exhausted and cold.

Bolts were drawn, the door opened an inch and a face peeped through the gap.

'I regret disturbing you at this hour,' said Robert, leaning forward, 'but I am cold and my horse is tired, and we must go many miles yet. Perhaps you could find it in your heart to give us a barn for the night, and maybe I can buy a little food?'

The door creaked open further, revealing a tall, handsome woman, strong and glowing with country health. She looked at Robert and smiled, then stood back.

'The horse can certainly be sheltered in the stable, sir, but not you,' she said. 'You must dry off by the fire, and be welcome.' She turned and shouted back into the house, 'Idris, come 'ere, take this gentleman's horse to the shippon. See it's fed and warm.'

A sturdy-looking boy, about sixteen years old, came to the door with a lantern. He nodded a welcome to Robert, glanced at the weather and, putting the lantern down, struggled into a rough coat. Ready for the elements, he took the horse to lead her to the shippon and settle her for the night – by the light of the boy's lantern, Robert could see that the shippon looked a warm and cosy place, so he stepped into the house for the night.

The dimly lit hall opened onto a large room with a fire roaring from a massive inglenook. Two long settles adjoined the fire, and a man sat sprawled on one of them. His dark hair was cropped in a rough-and-ready country way, and his cheery face was tanned like leather. He lay slumped back, one foot resting on a wolfhound stretched out on a mat of rushes in front of the fire, with a candle at his elbow and a book on his knee.

Good God, thought Robert, *the man can read!* He began to feel very relaxed – here was a man he could relate to and a hospitable place to stay. He could hardly believe his good fortune.

Opposite, on the other settle, was a girl of maybe twenty years, a piece of needlework in her hands. She had the nobility of the older woman – her mother presumably – but with her own charm. She smiled at Robert, then returned to her mending.

He glanced at his new surroundings: a black pot was simmering on the fire, another hanging above it; a pair of chests stood against the wall; and a brace of hares dangled from the door. Bundles of wild flowers hung from every rafter, and the room was completed with a large table – set for five.

Although relieved to have found such a warm welcome on such a violent night, he was somehow troubled by that fifth place laid at the table. *It's as if they knew I was coming*, he thought.

'This gentleman seeks shelter for the night, Tom,' said the woman, touching Robert on the arm.

The man laid down his book and jumped to his feet. 'Welcome, sir, welcome!' he roared. 'You have come at a merry time, for soon we are to eat.' He grabbed Robert by the shoulders and shook him in the friendliest manner. 'I'm Thomas Barker,' he said, 'and you have met Sarah, my wife.' Then he pointed to the girl by the fire. 'My daughter Bethany. Stand up, girl, and say hello!' he boomed.

The girl stood up and curtsied. 'Beth,' she said shyly.

Robert in turn introduced himself and explained the reason for his journey, then Tom settled everyone at the table, although when Idris came back in after stabling Robert's horse, he warmed his hands at the fire before coming to the table.

'My son,' said Tom. 'One day Idris will be master here, but not one day soon, I hope.'

As everybody roared with laughter at the joke, Robert studied this most happy of families. Already the five places at the table bothered him less. The meal that followed was excellent, and so much more than he'd dared to hope for on this stormy night – there was a hare stew with roast potatoes, pigeon pie of a sort unknown in London, beans with turnips, and ale. Oh, the ale! With each mouthful, Robert felt at one with these people.

Tom wanted to know of the progress of the plague, and Robert told of the many deaths, and of the devotions of the few doctors who'd stayed behind to try and fight it. He told how the cats and dogs had been slaughtered to stop the disease spreading; and of the wagons sent out at night to collect the corpses from the houses with red crosses painted on the doors. He described the scenes at the burial pits where men worked with handkerchiefs tied over their faces, and the fear in every street of this terrible 'black death'.

His new friends listened in sad silence. Then more ale was poured and the talk moved on to merrier things. They discussed the good harvest that seemed certain, and the happiness that a successful year provided. Idris grumbled about their bull, and Bethany spoke laughingly of the village boys, who walked ten miles just for a glimpse of her working in the fields. Sarah frowned at such talk and noisily stacked the dirty dishes as Bethany blushed and giggled.

As the candles spluttered their last, Sarah, Beth and Idris cleared the table while Tom and Robert sprawled in the glow of the fire; with tobacco and more ale, they discussed the falling price of wool, and Robert's ride to Derbyshire the following day.

When Tom heard where Robert lived in Derbyshire, he laughed. 'What a coincidence! When I travelled past your village a couple of weeks ago for the market, a friend asked me to deliver a box of your clothes to your house for him, as he was feeling unwell.' Robert had sent some of his belongings to Derbyshire ahead of his own arrival. He smiled at the chance, overwhelmed by a feeling that his unexpected and delightful stay with this family was somehow intended to happen.

The warm and happy atmosphere overcame Robert, and at last Sarah showed him to his room. He thanked the woman for her hospitality, not even noticing the hint of sadness in her stare as she quietly closed the door.

Robert explored the bedchamber. The fresh straw in the mattress smelled sweet, and the rush lights gave a friendly glow to the dancing shadows. The chimney below warmed the room, and Robert decided that even in London he could not have been treated more royally. He fell into a happy sleep, his dreams of life, not of the black death.

He had no idea what the time was when he was roused by a gentle tapping at his door: Bethany – she had come to share Robert's bed. As they lay in each other's arms they talked. They talked until the first birds began their song, and as the first light crept into the room Robert fell into a warm and joyous sleep.

The cold daylight woke Robert, and he sat up and found Bethany gone. The room had lost its welcome now, and the warmth had disappeared in the dawn. The cosy bed of last night felt damp now, and the room was cold.

Anxious to be on his way, he dressed and stumbled down the stairs. But the ash was cold on the hearth, and the room had an unlived-in feeling. Robert felt somewhat disappointed and suddenly anxious to leave this strange, dank place. He called out to his hosts, but his words stirred no response. Where had they all gone? Even stranger, the dinner plates that Sarah had cleared were back on the table, but there were only four there now.

Four plates. And they contained scraps of rotting food.

Robert called again, louder. Silence. Standing in this cold and desolate room, it was if the happiness of last night had never happened. The flowers hanging from the beams were withered to dry stalks, and the two hares behind the door were awful rotted shapes, with bones sticking through their fur. And where had the flies come from? The door creaked open and he stepped out into the cold morning.

He did not notice the red cross scrawled on the door.

He did not see the four unmarked graves, did not smell the decaying wolfhound sprawled over the biggest grave.

He went to the shippon and was saddened to see his mare there, shivering without straw or feed – she was even still saddled and bridled. Parts of the shippon roof had fallen in, and the place did not look at all cosy, like it had the night before. Robert looked around for oats or hay, but there was neither.

'Tom! Idris!' he shouted once more. Again he received no answer. Bewildered, he climbed into the saddle. Then he called out what was really on his mind and in his heart: 'Beth!'

His calls disturbed the crows in the trees, but there was no sight nor sound of the girl and Robert was overcome by a feeling of uneasiness and dread. The rain was gone and the sun was warm, so he took up the reins and urged his mare away, turning in his saddle to take a last look at his refuge. The stone building was dim in the mist and already settling into its fold in the landscape. He thought fondly of the people, but he was still troubled by the five places set for dinner and the sinister quiet of the morning.

When he arrived at his house in Derbyshire, he saw the box of clothes that Tom Barker had delivered. So he was able, for the first time in days, to change out of his travel-stained things. Warm again, he finally settled by his own fire with a glass of wine and a pipe. Home.

He awoke the next day, relieved to be back in the village. Sitting by the fire later, he thought over the strange events of the earlier days. There was a small blackish

lump on his arm, which he stroked thoughtfully with his middle finger as he gazed out of his window at the beautiful rolling countryside. He sneezed, and planned his next few days. Although aching, feeling a little sick, and very tired from his long ride, Robert felt very happy to have escaped from London.

Escaped, to the village of . . . Eyam.

A note about *Escape*

If you have heard of Eyam, I apologise for thinking you haven't.

If you haven't, then read on.

Eyam is a village in Derbyshire. It is very beautiful and it is set in the most splendid landscape. It is real and you can go there today, as I myself did some years ago.

The story goes that during the plague that caused so many deaths in London, most of the rest of England was unaffected. However, a chest of clothes was brought from London to Eyam, and the plague was hiding in that chest. Whole families died of the plague brought in that chest of clothes.

To prevent the plague spreading, the people who lived in Eyam then sealed themselves off from the rest of the world, going no further than their village boundaries. Food was delivered from surrounding farms and left at the boundary, where the villagers would collect it, leaving money in payment at the same spot. They lived like this until the plague ended. Sacrificing themselves in this way, they prevented the plague from spreading to the rest of Northern England.

When I visited Eyam, I started to imagine the progress of

that ill-fated chest of clothes, and the characters in this story came to life in my head.

If you are lucky enough to be able to visit Eyam now, you may be saddened to see the names of many of the people who died of the plague on the doors and gateposts of some of the older houses. It is sometimes still called 'The Plague Village'.

FRIENDS

Felicity Honor Penhaligan had no friends.

There were several reasons for this. At little school, one reason was that nobody could *spell* 'Felicity Honor Penhaligan' – that was why she never got any Christmas cards, or invitations to anything.

Felicity could not spell her own name either; neither could Auberon Penhaligan, her brother, who also had no friends for much the same reason. (Even *I* get bored trying to spell that mouthful, for either child.) But now you know Felicity's real name, we can call her by her pet name, Fliss.

Auberon was another difficult name, and Auberon hated it because it had sounded very like the name of one of the fairies from Shakespeare's *A Midsummer Night's Dream*. So *he* shortened Auberon to Ron. His mother, however, considered 'Ron' to be common so, after many arguments, Auberon agreed to be called Tim, which pleased everyone.

Another reason for Fliss, and indeed Tim, having no friends was because they were frightfully rich. They lived in the part of town full of old, rich people, and their house was huge with a large garden surrounded by a big wall – 'To keep out all of the common people,' their mum said.

It was strange that they lived like this because Mr and Mrs Penhaligan were slightly common themselves. Had they had no money, they would have been thought very common indeed. Mr Mudslop (that was his name, before he changed it to get into the golf club) had made his money out of making very cheap pet foods, while Mrs Penhaligan had given up her career running a hot-dog stand and married him shortly after he became rich.

Anyway, the high garden wall resulted in Tim and Fliss leading rather solitary lives.

When Fliss was old enough to go to school, the other children didn't like her because she was a show-off and talked about her big house, big garden and big wall all day. Yet another reason for her having no friends was that she was unusually bright, and there was no way that the other children could ever stop Fliss being top at everything, even Games. There was a lot of jealousy – after all, nobody likes a smarty-pants!

When Fliss went to big school, things were not much different for her. By this time she had become used to sitting alone at a desk for two, sitting in the dinner hall alone at the end of a table, and playing by herself at playtime. Well, she didn't really *play* by herself – she just stood around looking at the other children playing, and wondered what it would be like to have a friend.

Then one day, Fliss went to her desk and found someone sitting in the normally empty chair beside her own seat. She approached cautiously, as though drawing attention to herself might make the new girl move away. She lifted her half of the desk lid and shuffled her books, then glanced slyly at the new girl, who simply stared ahead.

The girl wore the same uniform as everyone else, but this girl's uniform had no creases or dirty marks on it at all – everything was perfect. Now curious about her, Fliss banged down the lid to try and get a response from the girl, but she didn't move.

Now Fliss studied her neighbour more intensely. The girl was pale, with almost white skin, and a small neat nose and mouth. The strange thing about her mouth was that her lips were almost the same colour as the rest of her face, and her pale face then merged easily into her almost white and perfectly straight hair.

'Hello!' said Fliss.

The girl turned her head and stared. Her eyes were pale, but ringed with a dark shadow. A faint smile twitched, but then she slowly turned away and stared ahead again.

Fliss was unruffled by this behaviour; since most children ignored her, this was nothing new. But what *was* new was that when everyone stood up for register, the new girl remained seated, and nobody seemed to notice. And when the names were called, there was no name called for her.

As the teacher rambled on about the sewage revolution in English seaside towns, Fliss suddenly felt cold fingers entwine with hers and she glanced sideways – but the new girl was still staring straight ahead. Fliss snatched her hand away. She wanted a friend, yes, but those cold fingers had sent a chill up her spine. She tried to smile at the girl again, but once more got no response.

At lunch time, the new girl followed Fliss into the dinner hall and sat by her at the table, although nobody offered her any food, and she didn't ask for any.

The afternoon lessons were just as strange as those in the morning. The girl didn't join in anything. It was almost as if she wasn't there and Fliss was becoming quite uneasy with her new companion – it was like *having* a friend and *not* having a friend at the same time. Like having a shadow that was not quite right.

Fliss decided that she preferred having no friends to this odd, cold girl and it was a relief when the bell went. She said a quick 'goodbye' to the girl and rushed outside to her mum's car and jumped in.

Then she screamed – the new girl was on the back seat! Mum asked her what was wrong but didn't mention the extra passenger, and the hideous truth dawned on Fliss . . . she was the only one who could see the girl.

The drive home was like a nightmare. All the time, Fliss could see the unsmiling white face in the mirror. 'Who *are* you?' she gasped.

'How do you mean, poppet?' said Mum, her eyes fixed on the road.

'Nothing!' said Fliss, glaring into the mirror.

When they swished through the big gates, and stopped outside the house, she jumped out and ran over to Tim, who was kicking a ball against the wall. She stood by her brother and stared at the car. She could see that strange white face watching from the back seat as Bloater, her dad's assistant, drove the car away to the garage.

'Tim,' said Fliss, 'do you believe in ghosts?'

'Course,' replied her brother. 'They're all over the place. Loads of 'em, especially in your bedroom.'

'I'm serious,' said Fliss. 'This is important.'

'Who's kidding?' retorted Tim. 'Don't be frightened of 'em though, cos if they can walk through walls they can't strangle you, cos their hands would go straight through your neck. You couldn't feel 'em, right?'

Fliss always thought Tim was right about everything, but he was wrong about ghosts – she had *felt* those cold little fingers grab hers!

At tea time, the family chattered as usual. Dad told everyone how much money he had made that day, Mum talked about how much money she had spent, and Tim asked Dad if he could lend Chelsea – the football club he supported – some money to buy an Italian midfielder, as they had just lost an important match.

Fliss said nothing; she just stared at the strange pale girl standing by the door, watching her. The presence of the girl was becoming unnerving, and Fliss was beginning to feel quite scared. Was something *horrible* going to happen? What was it going to be like later when it got dark?

If events so far had been scaring her, Fliss then discovered that there are worse aspects to being haunted. She rushed to the loo and bolted the door, only to find the girl standing there by the toilet paper.

'Go away!' screamed Fliss, sitting on the loo, leaning forward, her dress pulled over her knees. 'Go away!' The girl just stared and handed her the toilet paper, but Fliss found it quite difficult to use it with someone watching her.

She stayed up late that night, until the television programmes became unsuitable for children. All evening,

the new girl sat next to Fliss. Again, she tried to hold hands, and again Fliss pulled away in horror. The cold touch made her skin crawl.

'Can I sleep in your room tonight?' she asked her brother.

'Why?' asked Tim.

Fliss had no answer. 'Cos I'd like to tell you something,' she said lamely.

'No!' snapped Tim. 'Tell me in the morning.' And off he went to bed, before Fliss could ask him again.

Fliss thought she knew what to expect next, but when she opened her bedroom door the room was empty. She looked in the wardrobe and under the bed, but, no, she was alone. Her heart soared – it was as if a great weight had been lifted. Happily she undressed, pulled on her pyjamas and sprang into bed. She read for a while, but was too distracted to concentrate – all she could think about was the appearance, then thankfully the disappearance, of the new girl – so she turned out the light and snuggled under her duvet.

The pale girl's face peered at her from the other pillow in a ghostly glowing light and Fliss screamed and leaped out of bed.

Her scream brought the others running, Bloater carrying a heavy walking stick. Fliss pointed a shaking finger at the white head on her pillow.

Her mother cuddled her daughter. 'Is it an icky wicky dream?' she clucked.

'No,' sobbed Fliss. 'It's an icky wicky ghost.'

Dad patted her hair, while Bloater poked the curtains with his stick. 'No ghosts here,' they all said.

Grown-ups are totally useless when you want them, thought Fliss, clinging to Mum.

'Leave your light on, poppet,' said Dad generously.

Left alone with the new girl again, Fliss dimmed the light, but left it on. One thing was for certain – she was not getting into bed with that weird thing. Pulling on her dressing gown, she grabbed a pillow and stomped downstairs, intending to spend the night on a settee. But when she got there, the girl was standing sadly in the sitting room.

Fliss started shaking. The blank white face and dark ringed eyes seemed to be everywhere now, even when she wasn't even looking at the girl – they were just in her head, and she could still feel the icy grip of the girl's hand, although they were no longer touching. She felt defeated; felt that nothing could be done to make the new girl go away. She cowered on the settee and sobbed. The new girl crouched by her side and her cold fingers stroked Fliss's hair.

Fliss looked up with tear-stained eyes. 'Why are you doing this to me?' she moaned.

The new girl stared, then she smiled and spoke for the first time. 'You have no friends,' she said, her voice thin and unearthly, 'and you wish that you had. Well, I like you, and I will be your friend. I will always be with you. I will never, never, *never* leave you.'

'Noooo!' whimpered Fliss, collapsing to her knees. 'I don't want a ghost for a friend. I don't want a *dead* friend. What do you *want* with me?'

'I'm not *dead*,' whispered the apparition. 'I have never *been* alive, but I *want* to live! *And I want your body!*'

A note about *Friends*

This story is inspired by my memory of going to a strange school, my first school, when I didn't know anybody. So I know what it's like to feel lonely. I had an imaginary friend then, who I soon grew bored of, but he's never really left me alone . . .

To be without friends is the horriblest thing in the whole world. That's what I thought at the time. But I began to wonder what could be worse . . .

What if there was someone who never left you alone (and he wasn't just in your imagination)?

What if it was someone no one else could see?

Like a ghost, perhaps?

There are lots of stories about people who have died – but aren't people who have never been alive just as scary?

GARDEN

Once every year, the twins – Sophie and Jack – went to stay with their uncle on his island.

Well, not just *his* island; other people lived there too, but not many. Those who did mainly belonged to the sea – they fished for a living, and sometimes rented their boats to other people who loved the sea.

The island wasn't easy to get to. First you had to take a plane to the capital on the mainland, then a bus to the port, and then a steamer. With all the travel and waiting around, the best part of a day passed before you were on Paul's Island – Uncle Paul called it that and so did the twins. No one else did, though sometimes the postman came from the mainland with a letter addressed to *Paul Martin, Paul's Island* – the post office was happy with the joke, and liked that address.

Uncle Paul was a writer and lived like one. His house was the biggest on the island. A comfortable home, untidy but with lots of rooms, the house was always filled with sun and good food. Outside, the garden was large, and mostly happy to look after itself, which was fortunate since Uncle Paul loved gardens but disliked gardening. Every day he would sit at his typewriter, tippety-tapping away until the sun dipped, and then he liked to sit in his garden and thank his lucky stars for his life, for it had not always been so perfect.

The time for this year's visit came. Uncle Paul met the twins on the quay, threw their bags into his car and took the three of them to a café for cold drinks. He joked with the man who owned the place and the twins bubbled with excitement.

At the house, Uncle Paul tossed the children's bags into their usual rooms; they didn't bring much with them as the drawers were already full of their stuff – clothes and books – from their previous visits.

Sophie and Jack settled in, then met up on the landing and went to look for Uncle Paul. He was easy to find – they just followed the noise of the typewriter. The tippety-tapping stopped and, for the first time, the twins noticed how beautiful the birdsong was.

Uncle Paul swung round in his chair and grinned. 'What can I do for you two?' he said.

'We thought we'd go out for a bit,' said Jack. 'Maybe to the beach.'

'That sounds like a great plan,' replied Uncle Paul cheerfully. 'Take a rod each and see if you can get a couple of fish for dinner. About six would be fine, as there are some people coming over who would like to meet you both.' He turned back to his typewriter and then, almost as an afterthought, swung round again and looked quite serious. 'Remember, you can go anywhere on this side of the island, but please don't go too far, such as beyond the mountain. Nobody goes there and there is nothing over there.' He stared at the twins for a moment and then turned back to his work.

Sophie and Jack nodded solemnly; Uncle Paul always gave them this warning at the beginning of their stay with him. The mountain was at the centre of the island. It was not steep, but rocky, and looked fun to scramble on, though of course the twins had never done that, as every year Uncle Paul had given them the same warning. When they had been younger, the twins had been scared of the mountain, in case ghosts lived on the other side. When they stopped believing in ghosts, they decided that wild animals might live there – after all, everyone believes in wild animals.

For a while, they sat on the rocks with the fishing rods, but they must have misunderstood something important about what fishing was, because they caught nothing. They didn't even see a fish in the clear water so they finally lost interest. As the light was fading, they looked longingly up at the mountain, wondering what adventures could be had on the other side and Jack nudged Sophie, and whispered, 'Tomorrow, we could go up there and have a peek.'

The girl nodded eagerly – that's what they'd both been thinking about all day.

Uncle Paul's friends turned out not to want to meet the twins at all; they just wanted to sit in the garden with wine, watching the moths dance around the candles, talking about the old days. As there were no freshly-caught fish to eat, Uncle Paul had made pasta. When the twins had finished their supper they went to bed, leaving the old friends to themselves, talking, and enjoying Uncle Paul's garden.

Tired, happy and excited about tomorrow's adventure, Sophie and Jack made their plans . . .

Uncle Paul was up first, and when the twins tumbled down to breakfast he had already been to the village for fresh bread and pastries. They crammed down their food, grabbed their bathing things, took the fishing rods again, and set off.

Of course, the rods and bathers were only to make Uncle Paul think they were going to the beach as they didn't want him to worry. Hiding them under some bushes, they raced towards the foot of the mountain.

The day was hot, as usual, but as they climbed higher, a welcome breeze cooled the air. The twins were enjoying their scramble; the rocks were perfect – difficult, but not dangerous. In less than an hour they were standing on the top. Looking down from their viewpoint they could see that the landscape was very strange. On Uncle Paul's side it was green, with trees and beautiful flowers. But on the forbidden side nothing grew. The white rocks simply tumbled down to the narrow sandy beach, and even the sea looked less interesting.

'Uncle Paul was right,' panted Sophie. 'There's nothing there.'

'Except that!' said Jack, pointing to a wooden shack, built where the rocks met the sea. 'Let's go and look.'

'I think we should go back,' replied Sophie. 'I don't like it over here. It's so quiet and deserted.'

But her brother had already begun to slither down the mountain so, against her better judgement, she followed him and the twins arrived at the shack.

It was quite big with scraps of sky-blue paint on the window frames hinting at years of neglect. Creeping round to the front, Jack and Sophie found a veranda facing the sea, and on the veranda sat an elderly man in an old cane chair that also had flakes of sky-blue paint on it.

The twins studied him. The man was very old and had a white beard. He was wearing a white shirt and white canvas trousers, but his clothes were dusty and badly mended.

'Hello,' said Sophie tentatively.

The old man did not look round, but nodded. He was staring out to sea.

The twins introduced themselves, and the old man listened intently. Then he told them how he had always lived in this place, at one time with his family. Everyone was gone now, and for years he had been the only living being on this side of the mountain. He talked of fishing and rare visits from friends, and of his happiness, living where he had always lived. He talked of peace and memories.

'But don't you get bored?' asked Jack, always the one to get to the point.

The old man smiled. '*Bored?*' he murmured. 'How could I be bored? I have my garden.'

The twins looked around. They could see no garden, only sand and a few white rocks, going down to the sea.

'*What* garden?' asked Sophie.

The old man smiled. 'Why, *this* garden. *My* garden!'

The twins looked again. There was no garden, only rock and white sand.

'I've been a gardener my whole life,' went on the old man, 'and my garden is my greatest joy.' He pointed with his stick. A white stick.

'He is blind!' whispered Sophie, and her brother nodded. They stared at the barren beach in silence, then

Sophie spoke softly and touched the old man's hand. 'It's a very beautiful garden,' she said, and the old man smiled.

'Ah well,' said Jack briskly, 'we must be off. We have a big climb back, and our uncle will be wondering where we are.'

'You will come again?' said the old man, turning in his chair.

'Tomorrow,' promised the girl.

The old man turned happily back to his garden, as the twins crept away.

'Why d'you think Uncle Paul didn't want us to climb over the mountain?' Sophie asked her brother as they hurried home.

'Dunno. He probably just wants to know we're not too far from home. I can't believe we used to think that there were ghosts on that side of the mountain.' Her twin laughed.

Uncle Paul was pacing up and down when they got back, glancing at his watch. The twins had forgotten to pick up their rods and bathing suits, but he didn't seem to notice.

'I got some fish today!' he said proudly.

'But he didn't catch them,' grinned Jack, nudging Sophie. '*We* had the rods!'

Uncle Paul set about cooking the fish in a grill made from an old oil drum. 'There is no taste like that of fish straight from the sea,' he said.

'He must have got them from the village,' whispered Sophie.

But wherever they came from, the fish were very good. Uncle Paul asked the twins about their day, and they talked of scrambling over rocks, of the sea, and of gardens, without even mentioning the mountain. When they had gone to bed, Uncle Paul settled back to admire the evening sky.

Early the next day, the twins set off up the mountain again, scrambled down the other side, and hurried towards the shack. The old man was once again in his chair, staring towards the sea.

'Hello!' said Sophie cheerfully.

The old man didn't move, or appear to hear her voice.

'Hello!' she said again, louder this time. Again, there was no reply.

She touched the old man's hand. It was stone-cold.

'He's *dead*!' she gasped.

The two children ran as fast as they could back over the mountain to their uncle's house. He was tippety-tapping away as usual. The words tumbled out, as they explained their adventure and the death of their new friend.

Instead of being angry with them, Uncle Paul was horrified at their story, and saddened to hear the end of it. He jumped into his car and set off towards the village to get the doctor and some other men to help. They drove to the foot of the mountain, where the twins were waiting.

Together everybody made their way to the old man's shack. He was still in his chair, overlooking his garden, and now Sophie noticed that the smile that had been on his face when they left yesterday was still there.

The doctor examined the old man and pronounced him dead. All of the men took off their hats as a mark of respect, as the doctor wrote some notes.

'There's nothing else here now, kids,' said Uncle Paul, guiding the twins away.

As they slowly began to climb the mountain, they looked round. The doctor was standing by the old man's chair, still writing, while the men from the village were digging a grave.

When the twins got to the top of the mountain, they looked back again. In the distance they could see a low mound of sand on the ground near the shack – the finished gravesite. Some rocks had been placed around it, giving the little place some importance and the men from the village were now walking sadly away, heading towards the mountain.

'Did anyone know he lived there, Uncle Paul?' Sophie asked.

'Of course – he's been there for years. He liked his solitude, though. I think he saw a beauty there that none of the rest of us could see.'

'Do you mind that we disobeyed you and climbed over the mountain?'

Uncle Paul smiled. 'No. I think the old man wanted someone to see the place as he saw it before he left for ever.'

The weeks turned to months, and quickly the twins' sadness turned to memories. They fished and swam, and they sprawled in Uncle Paul's beautiful garden. The mountain was never mentioned, and the children didn't go near it again. Only too soon, the time came for them to leave.

On the day before the steamer was to arrive to take them away, the twins asked their uncle whether it was OK for them to go over the mountain to say goodbye to their friend there.

'Of course,' said Uncle Paul. His voice choked, and he turned away.

The mountain was alive with sun and the sound

of bees. As the old man had loved his garden so much, the twins each took a bunch of flowers for his grave. But as the old shack came into view, they stopped in amazement.

The land was still bare and rocky, the emptiness burned white in the sun – all except for the burial site. The outline of the grave was still clear, but instead of it being just sand and rock, there were two square metres of brilliant flowers growing there – beautiful green leaves and flowers of every colour, strange flowers that the children had never seen before, a tangle of rainbows on the bleak and rocky beach.

Jack stared. 'What . . . ? Who . . . ? How?' he stammered. 'How can this be? How can this garden be there? What on earth . . . ?'

Sophie smiled. 'It's his garden,' she said. 'Don't you understand? It's always been there. It is the garden in his heart.'

A note about *Garden*

I met an old man in a café once in Antwerp. The place was crowded so we shared a table. He asked me what I did, and I said I was an artist. We talked for an hour about art and he told me some amazing things about paintings, paintings that I had only looked at and never seen the true beauty of.

We argued and laughed, then when I asked him what he did for a living, he said, 'Nothing that would interest you. I'm blind.'

A blind man was telling me about art? It made me see the world differently, and my art.

Years later, I found myself living on an island. I loved it. So much so, in fact, that I chose to live on another island again.

So I put both of those truths together to make an *un*truth – a story. But what is untrue about a story?

HEAVEN

Albert Nuttall's declining years had been full of pain and disappointment.

The pain was the usual result of an over-active life. For instance, his knees wouldn't bend properly because of the football he had insisted on still playing when he had been far too old. As for all the other pain? Well, who knows what the cause of *that* was?

Albert had it *everywhere*. He had pain in his fingers, pain in his shoulders, pain in his back and, from time to time, even pain in his teeth. Albert felt especially badly done by with the pain in his teeth, as he only had two remaining – all the others were false. Anyway, he staggered about on his stick, grumbling about dentists and young people, who apparently were not as nice as they had been when Albert had been young.

The disappointment he felt was also more his own fault. He had married four times, all with the same result. On every one of his four wedding days, each of his chosen ladies had adored the ground he walked on. But on the day following each of the marriage ceremonies, the rot began to set in. Albert felt he had been a caring man and he had become obsessed with trying to restore love in his marriages, shouting at his wives and telling them how wonderful he was, and how lucky they were to have him. He was especially caring when drunk.

Try as he did, he could not hold any of his marriages together and, one by one, his wives had left him. Never for other men – Albert had cured them of that. No, they left him just to get away from his cruelty.

The lonely years were made bearable with a series of pets. Albert loved his pets, sometimes feeding them, but always administering discipline as he was under the impression that his cats, dogs and other pets understood his rules of cleanliness and obedience. In the main, his pets were cleaner than Albert himself, but whenever there was a little accident, he hit the roof and, just like his wives, the succession of pets all made their escape, often in suprising inventive ways – Albert always wondered how his budgie had chewed its way out of its cage, for example. And after that, he never kept tropical fish; on the basis of his past experience, he felt worried that the fish would defy millions of years of evolution and grow lungs and crawl away.

As the years went on, Albert was left completely alone, his only companions being his pain and disappointment. He went to bed early and tried to understand why a man as caring as himself could be

alone in his ninety-second year. How could such a blameless life as his result in him having to iron his own pants?

Christmas that year was a particularly dismal affair. He feasted on turkey burgers and Guinness, then rather than sit through films he had seen umpteen times, he decided to have an early night, again. He looked at the stairs. They had to be tackled.

The pain was excruciating as he and his stick creaked upwards. He had a mince pie to take to bed as a midnight snack, but he dropped it, and it was just too difficult to try to pick it up again. He tumbled into bed and turned off the light. Another Christmas out of the way, and another year ahead to get through!

Albert lay there, staring into the dark. Somehow, he felt curiously at ease. There were pictures in the dark: pictures of his life; his adoring wives, all four of them; pictures of happy pets growling and snarling on his lap; there were pictures of his old mum and of his dad hiding in the wardrobe. He remembered his days as a beatnik in the fifties, when it was OK to smell bad. He smiled as he saw his school, and recalled the look of hatred in his teachers' kindly old eyes.

In all it had been a good life, a successful life, a caring life. Albert smiled as he dozed off.

Tap tap tap.

He sat bolt upright, staring into the dark. At night, there should be no unusual noises. Although he couldn't see it, he stared at the door.

Tap tap tap! Someone, or something, was at his bedroom door.

Albert leaped out of bed. It had been years since he had leaped anywhere and he didn't even notice how fit he felt, how free of pain. If he could have seen himself in the mirror, he would hardly have recognised the young man in the old pyjamas. He opened the door to a fresh-faced boy dressed in a page's outfit.

'Mr Nuttall?' asked the boy. 'Mr Albert Nuttall?'

Albert blinked. 'Yes!'

'Born . . . er' – the boy consulted an electronic notebook – 'June twenty-third, 1910?'

'June 1910?' said Albert. '*No!* I was born in 1918.'

The boy tilted his notebook to the light, and squinted at it. 'Er, yes. The eights sometimes look like noughts. Sorry, yes, 1918.'

'Who *are* you?' asked Albert.

The boy straightened. 'I'm the Reaper,' he said proudly.

Albert stared. 'The *Grim* Reaper?' he breathed.

'Well, sort of grim as far as you're concerned,' smiled the boy. 'It's your turn.'

'My turn for *what*?' said Albert.

'For your Journey,' said the boy patiently.

'*What* journey?' said Albert.

'I've come to collect you,' muttered the boy.

'Collect me for what?' insisted Albert.

'OK!' said the boy. 'If you need it spelled out, *you're dead*!'

Albert gazed at the boy, trying to digest the news. Shaking his head, he turned and looked over at his bed. No wonder he felt young and pain-free – his old worn-out body was lying grotesquely spread-eagled on the bed.

'Can we talk about this?' he asked.

'Everyone says that,' grinned the boy. 'No point. Come on.' He stepped back politely into the gloom, and pointed down the hall. 'Chop chop!'

In a daze, Albert followed the boy – being dead, in fact, was a bit like being in a daze. The hallway was Albert's old hall, just as it always was, except it looked as if it had been cleaned. As they passed the bathroom, he hesitated. 'I'd better pop in here for a moment.'

'No need,' said the boy. 'Not now. Come on!'

At the end of the hall there was a door that had not been there before. By it there were two buttons set into the wall – a red one, and a green one. The red one said 'Down', and the green one said 'Up'.

The boy pressed the green one and the door slid aside, revealing a stainless-steel lift. They stepped inside,

the door closed and Albert felt the pressure of upward movement.

'It's *up*, then?' said Albert, studying the roof of the lift.

'Yes, it's "up",' answered the boy.

'I suppose up's Heaven?' said Albert hopefully.

'It is. The other place is "down".'

Albert smiled, happy that his lifetime of caring had been noticed in the right circles. He jabbed the boy in the ribs, wondering if all four of his wives would be there to greet him with open arms. Death was *good*!

'No mistake, then?'

'No mistake,' agreed the boy. 'The Final Committee never make mistakes. You are *definitely* booked in.'

The lift began to slow down, then shuddered to a halt and Albert held his breath as the door hissed open. When his eyes adjusted to the bright light, he could make out a group of figures advancing towards the lift.

The figures were of Albert's four wives. Not the miserable creatures they had been in life, though. They were different in death. They were all holding hands and pressing forward together, but when they smiled, Albert recoiled – their teeth were filed to sharp points! The four made grotesque kissing sounds with blood-red lips, and they surged forward, clutching and grabbing at

Albert. He tried to back into the lift, feeling cheated and terrified at the same time, but the boy barred his way.

'What's this?' Albert croaked. 'Heaven *can't* be like this. This can't be Heaven. There's been a dreadful mistake.'

'No mistake,' smiled the boy. 'This is *their* Heaven – not *yours*!'

A note about *Heaven*

Some stories are totally imaginary, nothing to do with anything, totally made up. This is one of those, except . . . the very idea of Heaven. When we're feeling a little sad, or just philosophical, we all wonder about: *What next . . . ?* And sometimes I think about not just what might happen to me, but what happens to everyone else?

During our lives, we meet thousands of people. Most of them walk into our lives, and out again. And when they walk out, where do they go, eventually? Do they all go to Heaven? Imagine getting there, and discovering that everybody you have ever met is there to meet you, and they have brought along everybody *they* have ever met, and *they* have brought along everybody . . . well, you get the picture.

So I started to wonder: is everyone's Heaven specific to them and the life they have led?

It may well be a wonderful place, but I can foresee some complications!

HOME

The bomber was a faint shape, firming up out of the mist as we trudged towards it. There was Kritzer, the pilot – a German, rejected by his country – three Poles and me. It wasn't that unusual for our crews to be made up of a mix of nationalities; our squadrons were quite international, unlike the rest of the RAF. But as the only Englishman in mine, I often had difficulty understanding the others.

The four ahead of me were disappearing into the mist when Kritzer turned round. 'Come on,' he shouted. 'Don't want to be late for Mr Churchill.'

The others laughed. Bogurski, the front gunner, scrambled up the ladder ahead of me. 'Tail gunners are always last!' he laughed as he squeezed into the plane.

When I was aboard, the door was slammed shut. I could only just remember how, three years ago now – when I had been at school – I had thought that this would be *fun*. Now, after seventeen bombing missions, I only felt *fear*. Fear, cold and loneliness. My bulky flying suit was like an eiderdown, hugging me so I could hardly move, so I could never understand *why* I always felt so

cold. Bent double, I struggled towards my place at the tail, settled at the guns, and checked their movement. In my head I went, '*Da da da da da da.*' Stupid, but I couldn't help it – it was my pre-flight ritual and made me feel better.

Once we were in the air, I settled down to the anxious hours ahead. Under other circumstances, my position in the tail, at the back of the plane, would be quite beautiful. I was enclosed in a glass bubble below the main body of the plane; I was flying, but couldn't actually see the plane. The constant purr of the engines was almost hypnotic, dreamlike, and I imagined the other planes strung out behind us dancing to the music of the engines. The only thing spoiling the dream was the nightmare of crashing to earth in flames, followed by a German fighter, its pilot watching over his kill.

Snap out of it! This is not a dream, this is a routine flight over the North Sea. Our target is a fleet of ships, assembled off Wilhelshaven. Some other chaps were there yesterday, but the job was not finished. They all came home. Today is another matter, different because we are expected. The fleet know we are coming, and so does a squadron of 109 fighters. Today, I may well have to sing for my supper.

'OK back there?' It was Kritzer, making sure I was still awake.

'OK, Skip!' I yelled in reply, trying to keep the fear out of my voice.

Kritzer called out to the others: Bogurski, Pilacki and Sawicz. Nose gunner, bomb aimer and navigator all answered in Polish; they sounded cheerful and, most of all, they sounded brave. These men were the best in the world, had fire in their hearts, but why, oh why was I there with them? I was too *young*. I should have been learning to foxtrot, not sitting behind four machine guns with my fingers on the triggers. I should have been at home, cleaning out my rabbits . . .

When Kritzer checked up on his crew, it meant that we were getting close to the target. The other planes had broken formation and were lost to me now, but the vibration from our engines was steady, and the others, judging by the laughter coming from the front of the plane, were in good spirits. They were singing songs and telling jokes in a language that I didn't understand and I was feeling sick now, not only from the fear and the cold (both worsening by the minute), but also from the loneliness brought about by the disappearance of the rest of the planes on the mission, and all talk in our plane being in Polish and German. The men all understood each other's languages, and also spoke English of course, but I suppose they had little to say to a tail gunner almost young enough to be their son.

I looked enviously along the body of the plane, and caught Sawicz's eye. He was a handsome man, of huge strength and determination, and he grinned and stuck a thumb up in the air. The simple gesture meant the world to me and pulled me back from the edge of tears. I nodded to him with a smile, and the navigator went back to his maps.

I turned my attention to the job at hand. I had nothing to do really, except admire the coast below, vivid in the autumn sun, and blow out my freezing breath in the way my Uncle Harold puffed out his cigar smoke. Uncle Harold had come through the First War without injury, so maybe I would come through this one? Thinking of him, I thought of Anne, his daughter, the nearest thing to a sister I ever had. I remembered the swing in our garden, and how Anne could always get higher than I could. Who's higher now, Annie, dear Annie? How she laughed when I told her I had joined the Air Force, and how she had bitten her lip when she had realised that I was not joking. It was Anne who had promised to look after my rabbits – for ever, she said.

A tearing crash jolted me back to the present, and the plane shuddered. Bits of canvas flapped wildly from the body frame, the wind tore more damage, and I clung to my guns, like gripping the handlebars of my bicycle.

'All right back there?' called Kritzer as he steadied the plane. 'Just a bit of flak.'

'All right, Skip!' I screamed back. I swung my guns down, looking for a target – one of the anti-aircraft guns that had just shot at us from the ground – but I couldn't see anything.

Trouble was, someone could see me. The day was too clear. I saw flashes from the guns on the ground. No sound, except for the reassuring throb of the engines, and every now and again, the plane shuddered. To avoid the guns sited around Wilhelmshaven, we moved offshore, looking for our target – a fleet of ships. Nothing! We scoured the sea near the port, but could see no ships.

Thank heavens! We could go home now.

Kritzer swore, in German; I didn't understand the words, but I understood the meaning. In English, he shouted an explanation. 'Yesterday's raid must have driven the fleet into the harbour. Our orders were to destroy them at sea, but to leave them alone if they are in harbour.' He swore again, the same words, then, 'I'm going in closer, to see where they are.'

Oh no, I groaned inwardly. *Our orders are clear, so let's get out of here. The kite's battered anyway. Any more of this and it'll drop to bits.*

The plane banked to the right, and I held my breath. The guns started up again and I squinted down at the port side, then blazed back, not really expecting to do any damage, more to show some resistance and to make sure the guns were working as they should. The ground guns threw up a wall of killing metal and more holes opened in the plane's body. Sometimes metal hit metal, but then metal hit flesh. A sudden blast of freezing wind tore along the plane – the front gunner was gone, his turret shattered!

'Bogurski!' yelled Kritzer over the roar of the wind. I heard no answer. I had long forgotten the cold, but the fear clung to me and my fingers were shaking on the triggers. I crouched low over my gun sights, hoping to make myself less of a target, but to my horror, four small dots appeared below me, growing quickly into the shapes of fighters. I swung my guns down – I needed to get them, before they got me!

As my machine guns spluttered, the fighters separated. Their pilots seemed to know that we had no front defences, and three of them swooped ahead. I blazed wildly at the remaining Me 109. It was so close now I could see the yellow centre boss of its propeller. The little fighter replied in kind, Perspex flew, and a sudden impact snatched the guns from my hands.

I turned my back on my tormentor, cradling my head in my arms, only to see Sawicz topple backwards from his map table. Ahead of him, the plane was lost in smoke, streaming back from the damaged nose. I struggled to free myself from my seat, but found that I could not move my legs. Blood was trickling into my eyes, and my right hand hurt. I was not aware of being hit, but I felt a dull thump on my right arm, and I winced and cursed the blasted fighter that would not go away.

At last, the Me 109 peeled off, his guns spent. I was alone, and I couldn't move. There was not too much pain, but a lack of feeling that frightened me. I slumped in my seat and, listening to the howling wind and the spluttering of one engine, I drifted into unconsciousness.

When I came to, the smoke had cleared. The plane was flying evenly, Sawicz was back at his table and, thank God, Bogurski was OK after all too. He was standing behind Kritzer, staring straight ahead. Ignoring the pain, I pulled myself round.

'Will we get back, Skip?' I gasped.

Kritzer looked round. 'I'll get you home,' he said quietly.

The cold was getting intolerable, and I kept losing consciousness. At one point I screamed – I don't know whether with cold or pain – and Kritzer looked back again.

'I'll get you home,' he repeated.

I squinted down to the ground. The landscape looked familiar – the higgledy piggledy fields and sleepy villages of England. But the plane was groaning now, her canvas skin hanging in shreds, her spirit broken.

'I'll get you home,' said Kritzer for the third time.

My pain was getting worse, and I felt as if I was hanging onto life itself. The plane was losing height, and I passed out again. A bump jolted me awake and I struggled to remember where I was, and to understand the situation.

We bumped again. We were down. The left side of the plane dipped alarmingly, and I could only hear one engine. We were careering along the runway, on one engine and one wheel, and I craned round to look at Kritzer.

He sensed my stare. 'I promised to get you home,' he smiled, turning round and then back to the business of handling the stricken plane.

Bogurski still stood behind the pilot, staring ahead, and Sawicz remained bent over his maps while Pilacki had come up from his position to witness the landing. It was the best show of flying I had ever seen – Kritzer had done the impossible, nursing this wreck home. We slowed down, the left wing crashed onto the runway, and the plane spun through half a circle and crunched to a halt. Again, my head throbbed. The last thing I could remember, before passing out once more was Kritzer, Sawicz, Pilacki and Bogurski all looking in my direction and waving.

'Home!' said Kritzer with a grin.

I became aware of new noises. The plane was full of people: Tommy Rudge, the armourer, Billy, Ted and Roland – three of the ground crew, who were engineers, I think. There were others, all shouting together.

'*Quick*, there's no time!'

'There's another one here!'

'How on earth did this heap get back? *Impossible!*'

I could just make out a medic, stumbling through the shattered aeroplane towards me. He turned to the others. 'Hey, there's one alive here!'

What was left of my gun turret was hacked away,

and I was lifted gently out and put on a stretcher. A young WAAF was watching in horror. 'He's only a lad,' she whispered to her friend.

The bodies of Sawicz, Pilacki, Bogurski and Kritzer lay in a line on the grass.

They had died over Germany, on an utterly pointless raid.

A note about *Home*

I had an uncle, who flew three tours – I think that meant about ninety flights – bombing missions over Germany in the Second World War. He was a rear gunner in, amongst others, a Wellington bomber. For years all I knew about him was an old photograph of a rather dashing young man in uniform, moustached and grinning like a film star. More than that, he was described in the newspaper as a war hero.

I was disappointed when I met him – he was a rather shy man, living on his nerves. Nevertheless, when a schoolboy met a war hero, there were sure to be questions. I had questions, but I got no answers. My uncle simply would not talk about the war.

In time, he reluctantly mentioned a few things. Firstly, he was scared silly on every flight, and he said his main memory was of fear. Secondly, he said that although he fired his guns many times, he could not remember hitting anything. Oh yes, and he was the only Englishman in the crew, and the pilot's name was Kritzer.

But I was always left to wonder . . . Where did his medal come from? And why did he continue to be my special hero?

OLÉ

The English children were bored with the little Spanish town.

Bored because there was no sea or beach.

Bored because the mountains were too far away to visit.

Bored because there was *nothing* to do.

They stared at the colourful poster of a bullfight in the café window. The poster showed a matador standing on tiptoe, his back arched, a black bull twisted around his slight body. In his left hand he held a small red cape, and in his right a long sword with a turned down end. He was bare-headed, his chin tucked to his chest. There was menace in the painting.

'Disgusting!' snorted Matt, glancing at his sister Emma.

She nodded. 'And cruel. It's not fair.'

'It's not supposed to be fair!' They turned to see a small Spanish boy, hands deep in the pockets of his grubby white trousers. 'It's not about *fair*; it is about the courage of the man.'

Matt frowned and pointed to the poster. 'Look,' he

said. 'The bullfighter has a sword, the bull hasn't. That's not a fair fight.'

'The bull has horns, and the man doesn't,' retorted the boy. 'Anyway, I told you, it's not about being fair and it's not a fight.'

'What is it then?' said the girl.

The small boy stood as tall as he could. 'It's an event, a spectacle,' he said. 'It's theatre, and it's history. It is not about the bull – it is about the skill and the bravery of the man.'

'I think the bull is just as brave as the man,' said Emma. 'Anyway, what do you know about it?'

'I know *all* about it.' The boy pointed to the poster and the three names printed in large black letters at the bottom. 'That's my father, Asier Balzola, the greatest bullfighter in all of Spain. I am his only son, he has taught me all he knows, and he says that one day I will be as famous as him. I am Paco Balzola.'

Matt grinned. 'You?' he said.

Paco grinned back. 'Me!'

Emma laughed. 'You, a famous bullfighter? No way, that monster would eat you for lunch.'

'Size has nothing to do with it,' replied Paco. 'One day I will be bigger, and even if I was as big as you it would make no difference, since that bull weighs over a ton.' The little Spanish boy shrugged and wrinkled his nose. 'I can't stand here all day though, telling you things that you don't want to hear. I must go now – my father will need me, we have things to do – but perhaps, one day, you will understand.' Then he grinned again and winked. 'After all, I am my father's son and I will be great one day!'

The English children watched him go, and then turned again to the poster. Emma tried to imagine Paco with the bull towering over him. The matador was staring along the blade of his sword, his cape touching the bull's nose, and she began to feel the oneness of the bull and the boy and almost heard the crowd cheering, pleading that one would kill the other.

'Get real,' she laughed, to relieve the tension growing in her head. 'Paco Balzola, the greatest bullfighter in all of Spain!'

At dinner that night, Matt and Emma told their parents all about their funny little friend.

'And his father is the best bullfighter in Spain!' finished Emma.

The waiter serving the paella stopped. 'What is his name, this great bullfighter?' he asked.

'Something Balzola.'

The waiter laughed. 'Something Balzola – you mean Asier Balzola? *He* is the greatest bullfighter in Spain?'

Another waiter joined them; he had been listening. 'I wonder what Dominguin, or El Cordobes, would say about that?' he laughed. 'If they have even heard of him.' The new waiter poured some wine. 'True, Asier is a bullfighter, but a long way from being great. Why, he is lucky to be alive. He is a sweet man though, and he adores little Paco.'

'They are a loving family,' added the first waiter, 'although there are only the two of them.'

The waiters finished serving the meal, chuckling all the time, and repeating, 'Asier Balzola, greatest bullfighter in all of Spain!'

The next day, the English children hung about the café, by the poster, hoping to see Paco again. They had talked the thing over and had decided not to mention the opinions of the two waiters, as they liked Paco and they wanted him to keep his dreams. In time, he came along, grubby white shirt, hands deep in grubby pockets. He grinned when he saw Matt and Emma, and hurried over to them.

'Guess what?' he said with badly concealed excitement. 'I told my father about you, and he said you could come to his next fight!'

Emma screwed up her nose. 'I don't want to see a bullfight.'

'Nor me,' said her brother.

'I know, I know, I know, I know!' laughed Paco. 'I told my father that you hate bullfighting, and he understands. He said that not all of us can be artists, for if we were, there would be no such thing as art in the world. He said you could watch him put on his special clothes before the fight, and ride in his car to the bullring, and maybe meet his friends. He said that in respect for your feelings, you need not watch the fight, or have anything to do with it. Afterwards, we could meet your parents, have a glass of wine, and you could tell us about England. I think you will like my father.'

'OK,' said Matt, 'we'll do that. Thank you.'

Paco stopped grinning and leaned towards the two English children, an arm around each of their shoulders. He glanced round, as if plotting something, and carried on in a whisper. 'There is just one more thing . . .' His voice was so quiet now, they had to strain to hear him. 'There is just one more thing you may like to do.' The warm day became heavy with the noise of crickets, and the very air seemed to wait to hear a secret. 'You may want to see some fighting bulls roaming free. We could go to the ranch early tomorrow evening and I will show them to you.' He paused and grinned. 'I will also have a surprise for you.'

The English children loved surprises, especially since the holiday so far had been so dull.

'Is the ranch far away?' asked the girl.

'Not really,' whispered Paco, 'and I can borrow bikes from my friends.'

It was dusk when the three children met by the café. The bikes were waiting, and they pedalled away into the gathering gloom. After three quarters of an hour, Paco skidded to a halt. 'This one is OK!' he said.

The English children stopped too. 'What one's OK?' breathed Emma.

'Over there,' whispered Paco, pointing towards the shadowy form of a huge bull. He was black, like all of his family, and the points of his horns were nearly a metre apart. Paco pulled a bundle from the basket on the front of his bike, and shook it open. It was a cape, bigger than Paco himself, yellow on one side, and red on the other. Paco gripped it with both hands, as if feeling its weight, looked thoughtfully at the bull, and the bull stared back, with no knowledge of what was happening, but suspicious of everything.

'Paco, what on *earth* are you doing?'

'You said I was too small for a bull,' said Paco, keeping his eyes fixed on the bull. 'Now we shall see who will have who for lunch!'

The English children watched in horror as the small boy, clutching the huge cape, walked purposefully towards the bull, who took a step back and pawed the ground. The rising moon was like a spotlight shining on a beautiful stage.

Paco stopped some metres from the massive animal and stood side on to it, offering up the cape. 'Aha!' he shouted. The bull did not move. Paco took a step forward and repeated the challenge. This time he shook the cape and the bull hesitated, then flung himself at the boy. Paco leaned back, hardly moving his feet, the cape enveloping the bull's horns as he brushed past. The boy swung the heavy cape round his body, spinning on his heel to face another charge from another direction as the bull skidded to a halt and turned. His next charge was fast, and immediate. Paco did the same movement, and again the bull thundered past.

Emma thought, rather than uttered, 'Olé!' Matt squeezed her hand.

Paco seemed bigger now. He waved to his friends, turned his back on the bull and strode away, dragging his cape behind him. This is what his father had taught him to do. Turning, he faced the bull again, this time holding the cape behind him. As the bull rushed, Paco swivelled round, holding his cape out to the right, causing the bull to swerve at this new target. As the animal thundered past, the boy swirled the cape over his head and walked away, arms in the air and cape trailing.

The English children hardly recognised their friend – he seemed to have grown up suddenly, and apart from his dirty white shirt and pants, he looked just like the matador in the poster.

The bull turned again and stared; he was panting, and no one would ever know his thoughts. Perhaps

he was beginning to respect the boy, beginning to understand him, even beginning to love him. Paco was certainly beginning to feel the same way. Also, he could see his father's face, smiling, and feel his hand on his shoulder. The English children watched with bated breath as the young Spaniard went through a procession of different moves. He seemed to grow in size until he was as big as the bull. But the bull's rushes now became more measured, almost more thoughtful. At the same time, Paco became more cautious in his movements, but more assured, and sometimes the tension between the two caused them both to stop and just stare at each other.

Paco went through all the moves his father had taught him, finishing with him dropping to one knee, with the cape arcing around his head. The bull's advance was slow now and it was as if he was working out a way to humiliate this boy, but Paco felt that he was getting the better of this contest and this feeling came through strongly to Matt and Emma, who had decided that the honours were even – Paco and the bull were part of each other now. Fifteen minutes had passed, and there was little else to do, nothing more to prove from either party.

Paco walked back to the English children, and the bull turned away. The evening was warm and very still, and Paco seemed more of a man now, and the English children felt very different. Perhaps the bull was different too.

'Did you see that?' he said. 'Did you see how I hardly moved my feet? Did you see that the bull ran out of tricks?' Paco was trembling and his eyes shone.

'You will be the greatest bullfighter in all of Spain!' breathed Emma.

Paco grinned. He was his father's son. As they pedalled back to the town, he said, 'This was a very wrong thing for me to do. If my father ever found out, he would be very hard on me. You must *never* mention to any living soul what you have seen tonight.' The two English children didn't understand why that was important, but each gave their solemn promise to keep the secret. Deep in thought, they did not notice the ride home.

Matt and Emma never saw Paco again. Their parents did not like the idea of the children going to the bullring in the bullfighter's car nor, in fact, having anything more to do with bullfighting. So, to stop the children feeling bad, as a family they drove away from that dusty little town to a new place by the sea, where there was swimming, satellite television and lots of things to do on the beach. The whole family had a wonderful last few days of their holiday.

At breakfast on their last day, their father was reading an English edition newspaper when suddenly he looked over his glasses at his children.

'Didn't you meet someone called Balzola, in the last place?' he asked.

The children nodded.

'Well, it says here that some days ago a matador called Asier Balzola was killed in the bullring. He was gored by a massive black bull, whose horns were nearly a metre apart. It says that nobody can account for what went wrong. From the moment the fight started, the bull, which had been bred on a ranch just outside of town, seemed to know what Balzola was doing. Normally, it says here, a fighting bull never sees a man on foot with a cape until it is in the ring, but this time it was almost as if the bull had fought before and learned what to do. Asier Balzola didn't stand a chance.'

Father peered again over his glasses at his two children, who were sitting perfectly still and were unusually silent.

A note on *Olé*

When I was a student in the 1950s, I took an interest in the history of bullfighting.

In those days, the most famous matador was Miguel Dominguin, and then El Cordobes, who cut his hair like the Beatles and was very popular. Both of these men are mentioned in the story, which I suppose sets it in those days, before football became more popular in Spain than bullfighting.

At that time, bullfighting was one of the few ways a poor boy could become rich. Sometimes they would go to a ranch at night and fight a bull for practice. This was of course illegal, as the bull learned the ways of the matador before entering the ring, giving him the advantage over the man. The more I learned, however, the more I felt sickened by the cruelty to the animals involved, and I quickly turned my back on bullfighting.

But the story of the poor young men practising bullfighting stayed with me and inspired this story.

PROMISE

When baby Rupert was born he rolled his eyes around his nursery and howled.

'He's hungry,' said Mummy, and she fed him immediately.

But Rupert wasn't hungry; he was terrified, terrified of nearly everything.

He was terrified of the pictures of Bart Simpson on his wall. In his tiny mind, he thought he would grow up to have yellow skin just like the Simpsons.

He was disturbed by his cot, because of the bars.

He was afraid of his teddy bear, in case it mauled him.

He was scared of the cat, because it looked at him in a funny way.

In fact, baby Rupert cried at almost everything and, every time he cried, Mummy fed him. So much so that he became frightened of Mummy in case she fed him again. When Daddy peered into the cot on Saturday – during the week he was at work all day and Rupert was in his cot asleep by the time he came home – Rupert burst into tears. Firstly, because he didn't know who this man was, and secondly because his moustache was bigger and blacker than Gran's.

The continual crying led to continual feeding. Which led to Rupert putting on the pounds at an alarming rate, which led to Daddy and the cat looking at him even more, which led to him crying, which led to . . . Well, you get the idea.

When it was time for Rupert to be christened, he panicked, not only because the vicar's shiny head and strange attire was new to him, but also because he was afraid of drowning in the font.

As the vicar struggled to maintain both his dignity and his grip on the hysterical baby Rupert, Mummy leaned over to Daddy and whispered, 'Are you *sure* Rupert's a good name for him? Shouldn't we call him something more manly?'

Daddy nodded and whispered something to the

vicar, who in turn nodded and, looking towards the heavens, said: 'I name this child Bart.'

As Bart grew up his fears grew with him. He didn't like getting out of bed, in case he fell out of the window whilst opening the curtains. If he survived that, Bart was afraid of breakfast. What if he tripped down the stairs and broke his neck? What if he choked on his toast? What if the marmalade was off and he got food poisoning?

If Bart survived breakfast, the dangers mounted up. School had always been an issue, and when he grew bigger Bart begged his parents to take him out of the local comprehensive, in case he was kicked playing football, or poisoned in the dinner hall. His father got him a place at Didcot Academy for Young Gentlemen. Of course, that was not without its problems either: Bart refused to play polo in case he fell off his pony and fractured his skull; and when in science class he learned that the universe was expanding he was so upset that he had to go home early with a nosebleed, in spite of his teacher telling him that it would not expand out of sight in his lifetime.

Although Bart feared almost everything, there was one particular fear that grew and grew – he simply did . . . not . . . want . . . to . . . die!

He had heard a lot about death, none of it nice.

And Bart had a lot to live for. He was rich (or rather Mummy and Daddy were). He lived in a big house, where he could sit and read poetry in a big garden, where things that sting were not allowed. To cap it all, Mummy and Daddy doted on him and would do anything to ensure his happiness. It was true that he was a bit of a fat lump, due to being fed whenever he cried, but that would pass. Take away a chin or two, and he wasn't at all bad-looking, either.

So Bart survived childhood and then his teenage years, by always looking where he was going. He avoided suspect foods like oysters or Bombay Mix, and he stayed in bed as often as possible.

True, a lot of people die in bed, but not when they are seventeen.

Indeed, Bart was in bed when he was gifted his salvation. He was under his duvet, trying to work out whether or not there was still enough air to breathe, and when it went dark, would he be safer if he turned on the light, and if he did that, would the light bulb explode and injure his head, and if it didn't, would it overheat and set fire to his bed and . . . ?

'Good evening.'

The voice came out of the dark and Bart jerked upright, all his nerves tingling. Had the murdering burglars found him at last? He had always feared this night. He fumbled for his bedside light and switched it on, but no light appeared.

'Aren't you speaking to me?' went on the voice. It was a nice voice, sort of silky, not the sort of common voice that murdering burglars had.

'G . . . g . . . g . . . good evening,' stuttered Bart, peering into the blackness.

Very slowly a shape began to appear in a sort of rosy light at the bottom of the bed and Bart began to make out the figure of a tiny man, crouching knees to chin at the foot of the bed. He wore an old-fashioned evening suit with tails, and a white bow tie, and his black hair was combed neatly back, dancing with oil. His face was as white as his shirt, his eyes two black holes with flashes of white.

Bart should have been scared, but somehow he wasn't. Who could be scared of a neatly dressed little man about two-foot-six high?

'Who on earth are you?' he said.

'I'm not often *on* Earth,' smiled the little man. 'I'm more often *in* Earth. Anyway, I have many names: Lucifer, Beelzebub, Satan—'

'You're the *devil*!' interrupted Bart.

The little man winced. 'That's a bit harsh!' he muttered. 'I prefer Nick. You can call me Nick.'

Bart was suspicious now. 'What are you up to here?' he asked.

Nick shrugged his shoulders and spread out his

hands. 'What do you mean, *up to?*' he said. 'I'm not *up to* anything. I know what you are thinking . . . Old Nick, Satan, the Devil, bad things are about to happen.'

'That's just about what I was thinking,' said Bart.

'No, no, no, no, no,' smiled Nick. 'I'm not like that at all; it's just that I've had a bit of a bad press over the years. You know, the Sunday papers, the Church, that sort of thing. No, really I'm an OK bloke.' The little man looked genuinely hurt. 'I just want to help people. Do you know, over the years I've developed this hobby of going around the world helping people? It's a bit of a tall order, but what I can do is make *one wish* come true for everybody – and tonight, Bart, is your night.'

Bart blinked. 'Do you mean I can wish for anything?'

'Any *one* thing, yes. But be careful – once wished, it can't be unwished.'

Bart's heart soared; he didn't have to think, as there was only one thing on his mind. 'I want to live for a good long time,' he said.

'Too vague,' said Nick. 'You must state *how* long.'

'All right,' said Bart. 'Could I live to be ninety?'

'Why not a hundred?' said Nick.

'A hundred and ten?' whispered Bart.

'How does a hundred and twenty suit you?' purred Nick.

Suddenly Bart hesitated. 'Haaaang on,' he said. 'I've

heard all about you; if you do something for me, I've got to do something for you in return – something like give you my soul.'

Again Nick looked quite hurt. 'Oh dear, my reputation again,' he moaned. '*Why* would I want your soul? I've got more souls than I know what to do with already. One more would just be something else to dust. No, as I said earlier, all I want to do is help. You won't owe me anything.'

'Promise?' said Bart.

'Promise!' said Nick, holding out his hand. 'A hundred and twenty.'

They shook on it and slowly Nick faded away, his smile going last. Bart fell into a happy sleep.

In the morning, Bart jumped out of bed and flung open the curtains. Instead of falling out of the window and crashing onto the path below, he found that the sun simply smiled on him.

He didn't fall down the stairs, or even choke on his toast.

He walked to school, not even looking when he crossed the road. He wasn't quite eighteen yet, so he knew he had another hundred and two years of life ahead of him.

At school, he took up polo, and lots of girls smiled

at him – he looked quite dashing on his pony.

Now Bart had a new life, he succeeded at whatever he did. His chins were down to one, his girlfriend was the prettiest and smartest in the school, and he realised, for the very first time, how wonderful life could be.

A few weeks later, his eighteenth birthday arrived, and Mummy and Daddy presented him with a brand-new sports car with two seats and a hood which went up and down at the press of a button.

'Be careful you don't kill yourself in it,' said Mummy, with a hint of concern.

'That's not going to happen,' laughed Bart, taking the key and jumping in.

His new car was wonderful, fast, good-looking and exciting to drive, and Bart drove wildly, first on this side of the road, then on the other. He swung round corners, waving his arms in the air. Corners were the most fun, the way the wheels screeched . . . except for the corner with the potato lorry coming one way, and Bart going the other.

Bart swerved too late. His car shot across the road, crashed through a fence – and flew over a cliff! As Bart rather stupidly was not wearing a seatbelt, he fell clear of the car and landed safely on a mat of new-mown hay.

'I'm OK!' he grinned. He *knew* he would be. Then his car landed on top of him.

Blackness.

Slowly Bart came to. He felt fine, but as he opened his eyes, he realised it was still black around him. He stretched out his hands to feel silken walls very close to him and a silken roof just above him and his arms pushed in panic. He was *dead*! He was in his *coffin* and the damp musty air was blacker than any black he had ever known.

He suddenly became aware of a weight on his feet. As he peered down, the air turned rosy, revealing Nick crouching there, smiling as usual.

Bart was furious. 'You *liar*! You *cheat*! You *phony*!'

Nick frowned. 'What do you mean?' he hissed.

'You two-faced twister. You told me I would live to be a hundred and twenty, and here I am dead at *eighteen*!'

'Calm yourself. I told you I am an OK bloke,' whispered Nick. 'You are not dead – the doctors only *thought* you were, since I allowed you a nice, long coma after the accident in which to heal. You *are* alive, and *will be* for another hundred and two years. I *promise*.'

Slowly Nick faded away . . .

A note about *Promise*

As a child, I often wondered why on earth my parents seemed to like me so much.

One reason, I supposed, was that I didn't ask for much. It was not that I was a reasonable child, as I don't think I was – I think I was as greedy as the next one. However, when I was quite small and in bed with the mumps, I was desperate for something to do and I found an old book of tales. Chinese ones, I think. One of the tales warned children of the dangers of asking for things, in case those things were given in a way unsuspected by the asker. Sometimes I wish I could find that book, for my own children.

In quite another vein, my parents drummed into me the importance of *always* keeping promises. These two parts of my childhood came together in this story, written many years ago in the 1970s. I was given a book of spooky tales to illustrate and, when reading them, I thought, *I could write one of those*.

And so I did. So a version of this story was one of the first things I ever wrote. If you read this one, perhaps you too may think, *I could write one of those!*

RAGGEDY

'What are you doing today, Jonny?' asked Dad one day after breakfast.

'Dunno,' Jonny replied, staring out of the window. 'I think I'll go down to the beach, see what I can find, maybe have a sail.'

Mum looked up. She always worried when her boy went out in his little boat. 'What's the weather going to do?' she asked.

Jonny hadn't a clue. 'It's going to be OK,' he guessed.

'Why don't you go with him?' said Mum, glancing at Dad.

'Too much to do,' muttered Dad, who liked to spend Saturdays worrying about Manchester City and building up to *Match of the Day*.

Mum bit her lip. She felt seasick just looking at the waves; she could never go in Jonny's little boat with him.

Jonny splashed through the shallows. The night had left nothing new on the beach, and the light winds and warm sun suggested that it would be a good day for a sail. He went back to the cottage as he kept his little dinghy on a trolley in the garage. He heaved the little boat over the shale, and down the beach. Running the trolley into the water, the boat floated off and Jonny dumped the trolley back above the high-water line, then began to rig his sail.

He knew what he was doing; he had done it many times before. The stub mast went in first, and he secured it in place with stay ropes. The red sail was laced on the gaff and then run up the mast, with the boom secured last. As the wind began to fill the sail, he swung the boat into the wind. The little foresail was run up the forestay, and flapped madly in the breeze.

Jonny pushed *Sunshine* into the shallows – *Sunshine* was the name that the boat's previous owner had given her and Jonny hated it, but it is bad luck to change a boat's name, and you need all the good luck you can get at sea.

He gave *Sunshine* a push and scrambled aboard. He dropped the dagger board – a sort of keel – into its housing, fixed the rudder in place and was off. Sitting to windward to balance the boat, he hauled in the sheets. When he had been younger, Jonny used to think that 'sheets' meant sails; it made more sense to him than calling the ropes that manage the sails 'sheets'.

Now in control of his boat, and of his world, Jonny settled back to enjoy the freedom that only a small boat can offer. He set a course for the northern end of Rat

Island and studied the shoreline falling away behind him. The beach was a thin yellow line, and he could just recognise Mum sitting on the sea wall of their cottage, waving. Jonny waved back to show that he was safe. Content, happy and safe.

He checked his lifejacket before pushing the tiller away, tightening the sails and speeding towards Rat Island. Jonny loved catching sight of this uninhabited island. Sometimes, on calm days, he'd moor up on the island and spend the day exploring.

As he rounded the island, the waves increased, as did the wind. *Sunshine* began to keel over, so Jonny eased off the mainsail and she returned to upright. The little boat hissed through the water, and Jonny had never been happier.

On this course, the next landfall would be America, so Jonny went about. He pushed hard on the tiller, and *Sunshine* swung round. He ducked down as the boom came over, and settled himself on the other side of the boat. *Sunshine* gathered the wind and lurched over and Jonny sat as far over the side as he could, the seas soaking his shorts. He had to let out more sail to stay upright. But without his noticing, the wind had strengthened considerably, and a bank of black cloud was rolling towards him, off the mountains.

As well as strengthening, the wind had also shifted – it was now blowing off the shore. To sail into the wind is impossible, so Jonny had to zigzag back home, but now he had sailed over to the wrong side of Rat Island to do this. Until that moment he'd felt carefree, but now – he had great respect for the sea – he began to feel a little nervous. However, he knew what he had to do so he went about again and, with the wind behind him, charged out to sea to get back round to the side of the island nearest home.

With the mainsail over one side of the boat, the

foresail over the other, and a strong wind behind, *Sunshine* boiled through the water. As the wind increased, so did the waves, and spray showered over the bows, drenching Jonny.

Now his concern was growing into fear. *Sunshine* shuddered every time she butted into a wave and to add to his problems, the little boat was taking in water, and Jonny did not have a spare hand to bail out. Releasing the foresail, he let it flap free and, pushing the tiller away, he hauled in the mainsail. The idea was to come right round into the wind where the boat would stay still in the water, the sails free, allowing him to bail out the water.

As *Sunshine* came round, however, a gigantic wave crashed over the side, filling the little boat with water. The wind gusted, and *Sunshine* rocked madly – then flipped over onto her side!

Jonny was thrown into the sea, where he had to watch his boat turn turtle, with her mast hanging below her in the sea and the little dagger board sticking straight up. He felt safe enough in his lifejacket as he battled over to *Sunshine* and pulled himself onto the hull, clinging to the dagger board. He was secure, for now, but still in a very dangerous position. He gathered his thoughts and looked around him.

Some two hundred metres away, he suddenly saw

the top of another sail. As the waves tossed, the boat
with the sail appeared, then disappeared. She was much
larger than *Sunshine*, with a rig that Jonny had not seen
before, but she was in as much trouble and he watched
in horror as the sea destroyed the other vessel. What of
the crew?

'Give us a hand, then!'

Jonny squinted into the sea. A boy, bigger than
himself, was clutching at *Sunshine*. His long fair hair
hid his face, and he held out a hand for help. Grabbing
the hand, Jonny hauled the boy onto the safety of the
hull and they stared at each other for a moment, both
clinging to the dagger board, and then the boy spoke.

'Let's get this thing upright, and we will be on our
way,' he said, pushing his hair back.

Jonny studied him, at that moment too relieved to
see another person out there to worry too much about
where he'd come from.

The boy had no lifejacket and his shirt and trousers
were too big for him and covered in patches, but there
was something about the boy that made him the captain
of this particular ship right now. He handed Jonny a
rope. 'Get into the water, and put your weight onto that,'
he ordered.

Jonny did as he was told – anything to get his boat
upright again.

The boy stood up and pulled on the dagger board. 'Keep your weight on that rope!' he yelled over his shoulder.

Slowly *Sunshine* began to right herself. The mast was just clear of the water when the boy stood on the dagger board and jumped up and down. The little boat swung upright, full of water. The two boys clung to the side as it rocked in the stormy sea, grinning widely.

'Thanks, mate,' said Jonny. 'What's your name?'

'Jack,' said the boy. 'What's yours?'

'Jonathan . . . Jonny.'

'Come on then, Jonny,' said Jack. 'Let's get the water out of this thing. You stay there.' He hauled himself over the stern and grabbed the plastic bucket, which was floating on the end of a line, and scooped water overboard. Both boys giggled as Jack aimed the water at Jonny.

'Steady on,' spluttered Jonny. 'I'll get wet!' They hooted with laughter as a huge wave crashed over Jonny. At last, the boat was almost dry, and Jack helped Jonny over the stern.

Jack took the tiller and the mainsail. The sail filled, and the boat began to move. 'Tighten that foresail!' he yelled.

Jonny did as he was told – Jack had taken command, and Jonny did not want to argue; he'd never sailed in weather like this, and Jack obviously knew what he was doing.

'Where to?' asked Jack

'Round the island, and head for the nearest starboard shore,' said Jonny.

The two settled to their course.

'What about your boat? Shouldn't we go and look for her?' asked Jonny.

'Nah, she's gone down. She'll be OK,' Jack called back over the wind. Jonny had no comment for this strange reply.

The wind still whipped the waves, but the boy handled *Sunshine* with authority and skill. As the wind had not shifted, they made their way home in a series of zigzags – tacks. The little boat seemed to know that she was in good hands, and she stopped immediately when Jack swung her into the wind. The shore was a quarter of a mile away, but the sea was calmer now.

'Why have you stopped?' asked Jonny.

Jack stood up in the boat and dropped the tiller. He pointed. 'You can do this now,' he said softly. 'The water's quiet, and the boat is dry.' He handed the mainsheet to Jonny and, as he did so, he squeezed his hand. 'You'll soon be home, and so will I.'

Without further explanation, he slid overboard. Jonny leaped forward to grab him, but he was too late

– all he could see was Jack's white face, disappearing, down and down in the sea. He was smiling, and then he waved, before vanishing.

Jonny sat back, staring at the spot where he had last seen his new friend. The sea became still, and he was aware of the seagulls laughing. The sea in their little bay was protected from the wildness of the storm blowing out by Rat Island. He did not know how long he sat there, but it was clear that nothing else would happen, so slowly he took *Sunshine* in hand and headed on the last tack home.

Pulling up the dagger board, he ran the boat up the beach. It took ten minutes to take down all the rigging, to secure everything and to haul the boat above the high-water line. He felt tired now, as well as saddened and puzzled. He stood, hands in pockets, staring thoughtfully out to sea.

'You weren't out in that?' Jonny swung round to see Dad standing at the cottage sea wall. 'Were a bit of a blow for a while, weren't it?' Dad went on.

Jonny smiled in agreement and the two of them went in for tea.

Jonny didn't tell anybody about his meeting with Jack, not until he met up with his friend Trudy. Trudy had been born on the coast – not like Jonny, whose family had only moved there a few years ago – and her dad was part of the crew of the local lifeboat. Jonny had been so troubled, seeing Jack vanish into the water, that he felt he just had to tell someone – so one evening, sitting on the rocks, watching the sun painting the sea, he told Trudy. He told her everything, and she did not laugh.

'You've met Raggedy Jack,' she whispered, her eyes sparkling.

'Who's Raggedy Jack?' said Jonny.

Trudy hugged her knees and gazed at the sea. 'Maybe it's only a story, but everyone says it's true,' she began, shifting round on her rock and fixing Jonny with an intense stare. 'Raggedy Jack was only fourteen and his dad was the pilot on this coast. This was over a hundred years ago now. And when the big sailing ships needed to get up the river, the pilot had to go out and show them the way, through the sandbanks and the rocks. Jack and his father used to sail out to the ships in their little cutter boat, and when his dad was on board the big ship, then it was Raggedy Jack's job to sail the cutter home. Believe it or not, he had done that since he was eight. But one night there was a big storm, and Jack had seen his dad board a ship. He got their cutter home OK, but then saw the big ship was in trouble, blown onto the rocks. He could only watch as she was bashed to bits on the shelf off Rat Island.

'Of course, Jack put to sea again in the cutter, looking for his father, who was drowned along with everybody else. He kept searching until the sea took his little cutter too, and Raggedy Jack went down with her. And seeing as you've just seen him, I guess he must still be searching.'

Both children gazed at the sea, thinking about its secrets. Then they got up and wandered home. At Trudy's cottage they stopped for a moment, and Trudy smiled.

'You were very lucky, you know, that Jack found you,' she said softly. 'He did the only thing he knew how to do – he saved you. I've heard he's saved others too. If a seaman is in danger, Raggedy Jack has to help. I suppose it's because he couldn't help his own dad.' Trudy opened the door of her cottage and looked back round at Jonny. 'But he had to go back into the sea; it's where he lives, it's where his boat is, and if he's away too long' – Trudy smiled – 'his dad worries.'

A note about *Raggedy*

When I was younger I sailed my very small boat on a very big sea.

Sometimes it was incredibly beautiful, sometimes it was gloriously exciting, sometimes both. However, no matter how wonderful sailing a small boat on a big sea is, there is always danger just round the corner. As the sea has no corners, under the sea was where the real mysteries were.

I used to sail around the coast of Anglesey, and those waters were notorious for the amount of ships that had gone down there. I can't have been the first to try and see below the waves and imagine those sailors, cabin boys and ships' cats still clawing their way through the water, trying to save themselves. And if they did get to the surface, wouldn't they know more about sailing than I did?

That's what I always thought.

SCHOOLED

The train was late again, and Bev was looking anxiously up the line, not wanting to be late for work twice in one week. Well, twice in three days really. He was deep in worried thought about his boss's state of mind when suddenly he heard: 'Beverly Cratchett, I don't believe it!'

Bev swung round to find himself face to face with Gary Barton. Gary's eyes were wild with excitement. Bev's were not.

Gary Barton barely had a friend in the world. His breath smelled, he was fat, he was rude – all inexcusable in a grown man – but the real reason he had no friends was that he was, and always had been, a violent bully. Gary's nickname at school (but only behind his back) had been *Gory*, because he had liked to make someone's nose bleed every day. He had been the school bully.

Gary Barton had made Bev's school days a misery. It had all started when Gary found out that 'Beverly' was a girl's name as well as a boy's. He used to shout across the playground, 'Oi, Missis Cratchett, where's yer 'andbag?' Everybody within earshot laughed – not because they thought it was funny, but because Gary would hit them if they didn't laugh. As Gary was the same age as Bev, Bev had had to put up with him throughout his school days. Every Monday morning Bev had crept into school, hoping to keep out of Gary's way, but the school bully had always found him. 'I shouldn't really hit a girl,' he would announce to the children crowding around, 'but there's nothing in the rules about *kicking* one!' Then, *WHOOOMPH*, up Beverly's pants.

Bev's dad had said, 'Go in tomorrow and hit him back. All bullies are cowards.'

That was one of Mr Cratchett's more stupid bits of wisdom. Wrong! All bullies are simply bullies and enjoy hurting people. When Bev went to hit Gary back, he wished he hadn't tried, as Gary's retaliation had been so severe that Bev could barely walk afterwards, so he decided against ever doing it again.

He had put up with Gary until he escaped to university, knowing that Gary was too thick to follow him there.

Now Gary put an arm around Bev's shoulders and gave him a squeeze. 'What are you up to these days?' he chuckled. 'Do you live round here?'

The arrival of the train gave Bev a chance to escape without answering Gary's question. Instead, he quickly said, 'I'm first class, are you?'

'Second,' muttered Gary.

How true! thought Bev.

To Bev's horror, Gary boarded the train with him. Clutching Bev's arm, he said, 'We must get together sometime. Are you in the phone book?'

Bev reluctantly admitted that he was, Gary stuck a thumb in the air, said 'Cool!' and headed towards the second-class coaches. Bev waited for a couple of minutes and then went to his seat, in second as well. He brooded all the way to the city. Surely Gary had no idea how much he *hated* him. He hoped he would never meet him again . . .

•

Bev lived alone. He had been married, but it hadn't worked out, although it had made him appreciate the pleasures of living alone. And he was doing well at work – his new boss had suggested that there was a chance Bev would be able to work over in Hong Kong for a couple of years and Bev had been thinking about it. Friends asked him whether he was lonely, but he wasn't. He enjoyed his cottage, his work, his hobbies and, most importantly, his own company.

He was enjoying his own company that evening in early spring, with his cat and his forty-two-inch TV, when his phone rang. It was Gory Gary.

'Is that Missis Cratchett?' he laughed.

'Bev speaking,' he said wearily. 'Gary?'

'Yes, ma'am!' laughed the voice on the other end of the line. Bev rolled his eyes to the ceiling. 'Seriously, Beverly, old son, I've been thinking, we really should see more of each other.'

Not if I see you first, thought Bev.

'After all, old school friends' – *FRIENDS????!* Bev's brain screamed – 'should stick together. What are you doing on Saturday?'

On the spur of the moment, Bev couldn't think of an excuse. 'Er . . . I don't think . . .'

'Great!' enthused Gary. 'Dinner at my place. Will there be a Missis Cratchett with Missis Cratchett?'

'No.'

'Great, just old pals together then. My place, Saturday about seven.'

Addresses were swapped and Bev hung up. '*Pals!*' he snarled. 'At least he seems to live alone. He didn't mention a Mrs Barton.' But an idea was beginning to form.

On Saturday, at seven precisely, Bev rang Gary's doorbell.

Gary opened the door. 'Young lady, you look gorgeous tonight!' he laughed. 'Come in, come in.'

Bev stepped into the hall. It was a gloomy place with watercolours of Egypt sneering down from the walls. He handed over the bottle of wine he had picked up at the supermarket and Gary put it on the hall table and forgot about it. The dining room was fashionably furnished, and the table was laid for two. *Definitely no Mrs Barton!* thought Bev with some satisfaction – his plan could work . . .

'Come and talk in the kitchen,' said Gary. 'There are one or two things that need a little care.'

All the talk was about school. Bev didn't say much, as he still couldn't really trust Gary. Gary, on the other hand, never stopped talking. He remembered nearly every name, and he seemed to think he had been well liked by everybody. 'Do you remember Limpy Taylor?'

he said. 'I ran into him a couple of months ago. He's done quite well for himself; he has a very posh antiques shop, and he earns more from being on television antiques shows than he gets from selling forgeries. We had a wonderful drink together. And' – Gary pulled a face – 'I kept calling him *Limpy*! And you know, he hasn't limped for *years*. Some sort of fancy operation. Good old Limpy. What a guy!' Bev remembered how when they had known him at school, Gerald Limpy O'Hara had one leg shorter than the other, and Gary liked to push him over – it had been easy, and Gary had found it very funny.

As they talked, Gary shelled two plovers' eggs and sat them on a bed of caviar. 'Ready now,' he said, and they retired to the beautifully prepared table.

The silver sparkled in the candlelight, and the cut flowers were perfect. Gary produced a bottle of red wine.

'*Châteauneuf du Pape* is one of my favourite wines. What do you think?'

Bev didn't know anything about wine. He knew red from white, but that was about it. 'Splendid,' he said, holding his glass to the light and squinting at the colour. It just looked like red wine to him.

'Gets its personality from stony ground,' said Gary, sniffing his glass. Bev smiled and nodded, studying his glass. *What rubbish*, he thought.

The plovers' eggs gave way to a rack of lamb with *dauphinoise* potatoes, finished off with champagne jelly and wild strawberries. The food was exquisite but the company was awful, and Bev could not wait to get away.

At the end of dinner, Gary suggested they sit by the fire and remember the old days. Bev acted out some yawning and stretching, and made his excuses. 'Gracious me!' he said, studying his watch. 'It's almost nine thirty!'

Gary looked dejected as he helped Bev on with his coat. 'Can't you stay a while?' he pleaded.

'I've enjoyed this evening immensely. But, work tomorrow!' said Bev, taking his leave.

'Tomorrow's Sunday . . . what do you . . . ?' began Gary.

'We must do it again. How about next Saturday at my place?'

A huge smile broke over Gary's face, and he nodded.

As Bev drove home, he thought about his evening. Gary was still as cruel and vile as ever, and Bev still hated him, just like he had at school. He had begun to think that his plan might be a little bit over the top, but after seeing Gary again he felt not. In fact, he felt rather pleased with himself.

Over the following week, Bev got in dozens of tins of food: any tins, the bigger the better. As he didn't have an old-fashioned tin opener, he bought one, the sort you poke in and waggle up and down. Then he went to a wine merchant to buy a wonderful bottle of wine.

'What sort?' said the wine merchant.

'Expensive,' said Bev.

'How expensive?' asked the wine merchant.

'Very. What's the most expensive you have in the shop?'

The wine merchant went to the rear of the shop and came back with a wooden box, which he laid carefully on the counter.

'*Château Haut-Brion*, 2009,' he whispered. He scribbled the price on a piece of paper and Bev went white. 'Would you like to sit down?' said the wine merchant. 'I'll take it back.'

'No, I'll take it,' said Bev faintly, handing over his credit card.

The week flew by, and Bev made some other purchases at the ironmonger's. Then he spent most of Saturday busying himself in the cellar.

Seven twenty-nine, and Bev sat waiting for Gary's arrival. There was still time to change his plans. No, there wasn't, for suddenly the bell rang, Gary stepped into the cottage, and handed him a bottle of *Châteauneuf du Pape*. Bev glanced at it and put it on the hall chair.

The dinner table looked warm and welcoming, and the two men sat down.

'I know that you are interested in wine, so how about a glass before we eat?'

'I liked the one you brought to my place last week,' said Gary with a nasty grin. 'A useful little wine – I cleaned the car with it. Is this one as good?'

'You can be the judge of that,' said Bev, and he carefully placed the opened *Château Haut-Brion* on the table. Gary stared at it in disbelief, licking his lips as Bev polished two glasses and then carefully poured the wine into them, gently standing the bottle on the table.

The two men sipped and Gary closed his eyes as the taste exploded in his mouth. The taste was magical, dreamlike, sublime.

'How did an ordinary little lady like you afford a wine like this?' he asked.

'I can't really *afford* it,' whispered Bev quietly, into his glass. 'It's just that . . . well, wine is my passion, and I spend every penny I have on my cellar. This is nothing compared to some of the stuff I have down there.'

Gary jerked to his feet, his eyes shining wildly. 'Show me!' he gasped. 'Show me your cellar, now!'

'Nooooo. I don't think so,' said Bev. 'I never take anyone down there. I'll get the pasta.'

All through the simple meal, Gary went on and on about the cellar, at one point even gripping Bev's arm in a painful twist as he pleaded with him. Bev kept changing the subject and rubbed his sore arm. An hour passed, and the wine was gone.

'I'll get another,' said Bev, standing up. 'We can try a better one.'

Gary jumped up. 'Let me come too, please!'

'Oh, if you must,' said Bev, releasing his shoulder from Gary's persuasive grip.

He opened the cellar door and stood aside, allowing Gary to go first.

Gary stepped onto the top stair, with Bev right behind him. 'It's dark,' he said. 'I can't see a thing.' Suddenly he felt a sharp blow on his right wrist, and the light snapped on. He was wearing a handcuff, linked to a stout chain that in turn was linked to a sturdy bolt in the wall. With a sudden surge of panic he looked at Bev, who smiled sweetly.

'Don't like it, eh?' Bev said. 'I wonder if you are as frightened now as I was for all those years at school. If you're not, then you've time to learn. I'm off to Hong Kong for a couple of years. At least you will have the time to remember all of the boys whose lives you made miserable.'

Gary tried to say something, but the words wouldn't come. Bev left the cellar, bolting the door behind him and Gary tried to calm himself. He went down the stairs and looked around. There was a sink with a tin plate and cup in it, also a sharp carving knife. At the far end of the cellar, there was a mountain of tinned food and a tin opener.

Gary tried the tap and drank the cold water. He looked at the food. 'At least I won't starve until I can get out of here.' He spoke out loud, just to break the silence. He went over to the food, but he couldn't quite reach it, as his chain was just not long enough. He stared at the food thoughtfully, then lay down on his back, and reached out with his foot. Still out of reach. His next plan was to hold the carving knife between his feet and try to drag some food over. No luck – still fifteen centimetres away. He had another drink of water and then sat on the stairs to think the problem through, but first he tried to chip the bolt out of the wall, only to break the point off the knife.

Gary tried everything, but the food was always just beyond reach. However, he decided that Bev couldn't be serious and anyway, as if a snivelling little wimp like him would have the guts to see through a plan like this!

He slept quite well that first night, sure that Bev would come to his senses in the morning. But when he woke up on the second day, he began to cry. The house was silent, and Bev really had left. What had he done to deserve this? They'd all had a laugh at school, he thought – it hadn't been his fault if the other kids hadn't been as strong as him and got hurt easily. Bev just couldn't take a joke.

After a week, Gary felt he was losing his sanity. Each passing hour left him hungrier and he lost track of time, and lost all sense of reality. He was so hungry he became obsessed with the pile of food, and one day the solution hit him. It was so obvious he should have thought of it before. All he had to do was cut off his hand to escape the handcuff.

He stared at the carving knife for hours before he started. The pain was worse than the pain of hunger, but he had to do it . . .

Gary kept passing out, and he did not keep track of how long he was unconscious, but he kept sawing away at his wrist. At last, after many many hours, he was free. The school bully lay on the cold floor and sobbed as the pain came and went in waves, one minute unbearable, the next a dull throb. Panting and whimpering, and slipping in and out of consciousness, he crawled over to the food and took hold of the tin opener.

But he needed another hand to hold the tin.

A note about *Schooled*

After leaving art school, I got a job with an advertising agency, involving my going to and from town on the train. Imagine my surprise to be clapped (too hard) on the shoulder and, on turning round, to find myself staring at someone I was at school with.

I will tell you nothing about him, nothing more than to say that he tried to make my life a misery. The early part of this story is true; the rest I made up. As I got on another part of the train, I vowed never to see him again, although that meeting did linger in my mind until it turned itself into a story.

Really, I should have felt sorry for that bully because he was a sad character. I believe it is the bully who has the real problem, not the victim.

In spite of that, I simply did not like him, and would never dream of asking him home.

Unless . . .

SMILE

I have often thought that on leaving university I should have taken up some easy profession – concert pianist, for instance, or footballer, or even a trapeze artist.

But did I? No, I followed my heart and became an art dealer. Being poor, I could not afford to buy art, or indeed to rent space for a gallery to deal from, so I advertised my services, offering to acquire pieces of art for those who were prepared to pay.

The bulk of my business was in supplying great works by un-great artists, or sometimes un-great works by great artists to those who wished to buy. On one occasion, I found a tiny scribble by Matisse, who had thoughtfully signed it, perhaps with me in mind. I made a good profit out of that one, and I was *almost* certain it was genuine.

So, I struggled along with my posh car and cheap apartment. It was an interesting life and it amused me. But oh, I wish, I dearly wish that I had never heard of Anton Barbes.

His letter to me included an air ticket to Nice, on the French Riviera, and the advice that using it would be of great benefit to me. I was tired of warring with an angry client in Lancashire, who claimed that the L.S. Lowry drawing I had found for him was not genuine, simply because it was drawn in biro (well, the great artist lived until the 1970s, and they had biros then!). He even went as far as to suggest that I had done it myself. As if!

So, a holiday was overdue.

At Nice airport I was greeted by a man holding a card with my name on it. Heading away from the taxi rank, I was taken to a helicopter and whisked along the coast to Monaco. As the Riviera, with its villas and beautiful gardens and coves, slipped by beneath me I dreamed of the exciting new world I had found. The helicopter settled down in the grounds of a villa, clinging to the top of a cliff.

I was taken through exotic gardens, past a cascade, to a terrace set with a single table and two chairs. A small man sat at the table, watching me carefully, and several Algerian gardeners paused in their work to watch me as I climbed the steps.

Anton Barbes was a curious man, ugly, with the most beautiful clothes. His age? Who could tell? Anywhere between fifty and one hundred. We stared at each other across the table, then Barbes smiled. I shook my head to his offer of a cigarette but, of course, accepted a glass of wine. His thin fingers stroked his glass as he gazed thoughtfully

at me and I was not sure what to say. The beautiful wine and the exceptional place instilled a sense of unreality in me. On occasions like this, the extraordinary could happen.

Barbes broke the spell. When he leaned forward, I realised that he had one blue eye, and one brown. He spoke to me in English. 'I would like to buy the *Mona Lisa* from you.'

I stared. I smiled. I remained silent. Could this be happening?

'Would that be possible, for fifty million of your pounds?'

'It would be impossible,' I replied, in a rather empty way. I had seen a beautiful part of the world, but I realised then that I had to get back to London and forget all about it.

Anton Barbes was in no hurry though. He poured more wine, and smiled at me. 'The impossible is always expensive,' he said, 'but always fascinating. The price I offer is surely worth your consideration?'

Barbes was right, of course, and he knew that I would think about his offer, once I became used to it. The wine, the warmth, the beauty of my surroundings and the company of this extraordinary little man made me feel easier with the idea. If there was a way, then I would only have to fulfil this one task and I could retire at twenty-three, and perhaps live like this myself.

The beautiful afternoon turned into a memorable evening, and finally, at a breath-taking restaurant in a medieval village, I agreed to try and steal the most famous painting in the world.

I lay awake in my hotel in Nice, and the more I dwelled on the problem, the more ways I dreamed of solving it. At breakfast, I felt very excited as I had the bones of a plan in my mind. The fifty million pounds had become of less importance than the fun – yes, the fun – of stealing a little Italian painting by Leonardo da Vinci.

From Nice I flew straight to Paris and headed to the Louvre museum. I joined the crowd gaping at the *Mona Lisa*. She looked shyly at me, and I felt almost guilty with my plan to disturb her tranquillity. Her smile had taken on a new meaning for me; it almost seemed that she knew what I was up to and, more importantly, was enjoying the joke.

I'd decided that the problem was not in removing the bulletproof frame from the wall – the problem was getting the picture out of the museum against the attentions of a vigilant staff, beating one of the world's most sophisticated alarm systems. So I'd decided to let the alarm do its business, and to remove the picture in another way. I would need to trust three people, and to find an almost deserted room or cupboard as near to my target as possible.

I will not bore you with the details of finding my three accomplices. It is enough to say that Paris is full of people ready to take a risk for ten thousand Euros, and a further million on completion. In cafés and bars, I found my three: an attendant at the Louvre, with dreams of a sailing boat in Brittany; a doctor, whose career was about to be interrupted by legal action; and an old man, gaunt and feeble, who needed money for his children's happiness in a world he had found so cruel.

The room was located – a small maintenance room, close to the gallery of sixteenth-century Italian paintings, where the *Mona Lisa* hung on a wall by herself.

I was ready to go.

My attendant supplied me with his spare uniform and copies of his keys. I carried them into the museum in a holdall, went to my small room and changed. Examining the floorboards, I located the two easiest to lever up and undid the screws holding these two sections down. The gap revealed was only about thirty centimetres or so, but adequate for my needs. The boards flopped back easily, without signs of tampering.

Now and again, I strolled into *Mona Lisa*'s room, mingling easily with the crowd. Speaking only schoolboy French, I had to get used to being an attendant, and be accepted as one.

I was careful about my preparations, and I wondered

if I was simply nervous about proceeding with my plan, but I knew that the best way to get into cold water is to jump straight in.

So the fateful day arrived. I had sold my posh car and my apartment and, adding that money to my savings, I made the first payments to my little team. I now had nothing but the promised fifty million pounds if my plan succeeded, or numerous TV appearances, newspaper stories and prison if it didn't.

I arrived at the museum early and went to my room to change. As usual, the crowds of visitors gathered to stare at what I had begun to think of as *my* painting. I stood around in what I thought was an attendant-like way, only moving off if a real attendant came anywhere near me.

When the time came for the gallery to close, the crowds were ushered away, and the attendants checked the rooms, one by one. Not wanting to be involved with the other attendants, I went to hide in my little room.

I passed a few hours with a crossword puzzle and a sandwich, and then peeped out. All was quiet, and in the dim lighting I crept towards my picture. She was waiting for me, her smile now welcoming.

I hesitated – there was still time to back out – but no, the prize was too big to walk away from. I pulled a hefty crowbar from my trousers and wrenched the picture off the wall. It came away easily and I grabbed it – bulletproof glass, frame and all. The alarms crashed around me and I ran for my room, but before I could get there a couple of attendants came towards me. I leaned the picture face against the wall and stood in front of it, then pointed wildly to the room I had just left.

One of the two attendants was my man, and he grabbed the other, rushing him past me. I got to my little room and slipped inside, locking the door. Taking the fragile wooden panel out of the frame, I wrapped it in velvet and laid it carefully under the floor, screwing down the floorboards, making sure to hide the frame as well.

Stepping out into the hall, I locked the door behind me. The alarms were silent now, but there was a hubbub of excited voices, and police and others were milling around. Nobody looked twice at me as I hurried out of a staff entrance. Still wearing my uniform, I slipped away into the night, went back to my hotel and changed into more comfortable clothes, then found a quiet café for pasta and a glass of wine.

Happily, I stared out into the darkened street, rejoicing in the importance of what I had done. I felt wonderful!

I walked on air for a couple of days and left the *Mona Lisa* in the little room, to allow a period of calm.

I enjoyed Paris, doing all of the things that tourists do until at last the time came for me to complete my plan.

I went back to my room in the museum, where I slipped on my uniform once more. I could not resist peeping at the *Mona Lisa*; she was still there, under the floor, smiling at me.

About noon, I left my room and met up with my attendant. Together we mingled with the crowds. The *Mona Lisa* room was closed off with a notice saying something about re-hanging, and disappointed visitors were wandering about. Occasionally a policeman sauntered by, but the urgency of a few nights ago was gone.

A frail-looking old man suddenly stopped in his tracks and, leaning against a window ledge, started to gasp and clutch his chest. He staggered a few steps and then crashed to the floor.

Another man – a doctor – kneeled down next to the old man. He held the old man's wrist and cradled his head, then looked up at the anxious crowd and cried, 'Get a stretcher, *now*!' He spoke into his phone then, looking at my attendant, said, 'Is there somewhere quiet we can take him until the ambulance arrives?'

My attendant slipped away and came back with a plastic stretcher, and the police held back the onlookers as we carried the old man to my little room. Locking the door, we acted quickly. The old man hopped up and we placed the painting on the stretcher, covering it with a piece of plywood. Grinning, the old man laid down again, and we wrapped him in a red blanket.

The doctor's phone rang. 'The ambulance is here,' he said.

The police helped us put the old man into the ambulance, and we sped away, siren braying. No one thought it odd that two attendants had gone too.

When we reached the hospital, I said my farewells and took a taxi back to my hotel with my picture. I'd arranged it that as soon as I had the reward money, I would transfer one million Euros to each of my three accomplices' accounts.

I had pulled it off! I had the *Mona Lisa*, the most valuable piece of art in the world.

Not wishing to be involved with public transport, I hired a car and drove down to Monaco. I enjoyed the drive; the weather was perfect, almost as perfect as my world.

Anton Barbes met me on his terrace. His stare was cold and he asked me what I wanted. I was taken by surprise at his tone and explained that I had his picture.

Barbes turned away and muttered, 'Take it away, I don't want it.'

I was stunned. 'I have the *Mona Lisa* in my car,' I stammered. 'You owe me money.'

Barbes swung round. 'I owe you nothing!' he snarled. 'I'll let you get away with your life this time, but don't you *dare* try a stunt like that again. The picture was not stolen! There has been nothing in the media about a theft, and my man in Paris phoned today – he has seen the picture, still on the wall. Get back into your car and take whatever piece of junk you've found away with you.'

My world spun. 'But . . .'

'Get him out of here,' snapped Barbes, turning on his heel and stalking towards the house.

I will always remember my drive back to Paris. It was like a dream, a bad dream. In my hotel, I propped up the painting on my bed. The smile seemed almost a sneer. I was running out of money, and ideas, for I couldn't take the picture anywhere else.

The next day, I phoned the Louvre to arrange to hand the picture back. No one seemed to know anything about any theft so, after some argument, I made an appointment to see the director. Not today, but at two-thirty tomorrow.

At two-thirty on the dot, I was shown into the office of an assistant director, a dapper young man oozing charm. He sat calmly behind his desk, fingers together, patiently listening to my tale.

'I have the picture in a safe place,' I finished, 'and with all humility, I implore you to take it back. I am not asking for fifty million Euros, only a quarter of a million, to cover some of my expenses. Oh, and freedom from charges. If you want the *Mona Lisa* back, the police must not be involved.'

The assistant director stood up, and smiled. 'Of course, there will be no money, *or* charges,' he said, 'and as for any picture you claim to have, well, you may keep that.'

My mouth was dry, and I stared at him in disbelief.

Still smiling, he said, 'I don't really owe you an explanation, but I will give you one. Come!' He left the office, and I stumbled along after him in disbelief. First, he took me to the *Mona Lisa* gallery. There she was, alone on her wall, smiling at her adoring crowd, as if sharing a joke.

The assistant director hurried me on. Down grand stairways and down narrow stairways, arriving at an iron door. He nodded to an assistant, who unlocked the door and swung it open. What I saw took my breath away.

Dozens of *Mona Lisa*s!

All on wooden panels, all braced at the back against

warping, all with a tiny crack running down from the top.

The assistant director stood, hands in pockets. 'The actual *Mona Lisa* was stolen over a hundred years ago,' he purred, 'and as we never got her back, we had another one painted. Well, in 1911 she went again, so a third was made. Since then, she is stolen every few years, and when that happens it is much more convenient just to pop up another one. So, to save time, we have had quite a few painted, just in case. I do regret all the trouble you have been put to over this and I can only wish you the best of luck in the future, and hope that you enjoy your painting.' He turned and beckoned to the assistant. 'Call a taxi for Mr Ross, will you!'

A note about *Smile*

It is probably the most famous picture in the world, and the most valuable. It was painted by Leonardo da Vinci in 1503 and finished in 1519 – all that time, and he painted no eyebrows. Apart from its age, and its painter's genius, the value lies in the mystery of the woman herself. Why was she so important to Leonardo? How is her smile so *life-like*? Who was she? What was the painter trying to achieve when he claimed after sixteen years that it was still unfinished?

Some years ago, I had some business to do at the gallery where the *Mona Lisa* lived. I was early, so I went to have a look at her. Like many before me, it crossed my mind to grab the little wooden panel and make a dash with it. I even asked an attendant how it was fastened to the wall. He didn't answer.

I didn't know then that she had in fact been stolen long ago, in 1911 (returned to the Louvre twenty-eight months later). When I discovered this my story began to form. The people I met at the Louvre had hinted at the world of delights and mysteries that existed below the galleries, and my story became a possibility, but no, no, no, no, these things can't happen.

Impossible.

TED

Maisie hated car-boot sales.

Her mum and dad loved them though, so every Sunday she was dragged miles away, to some windswept field, to look at tables covered with old junk.

Who on earth buys this stuff? she thought, poking a pair of sweat-stained Nikes, one with the tick hanging off. *Dad would, that's who.*

And he did. 'That's easily fixed,' he said. Mum nodded, peeping inside a greasy old sandwich toaster.

While Mum and Dad were arguing about whether or not they had space for an outdated keep-fit machine (neither of them had ever been fit in the first place), Maisie slipped away to look for treasures of her own. She had seen things on the *Antiques Roadshow* that had been bought at car-boot sales for ten pence, and were now worth millions of pounds. She was looking for something like that.

She had ten pence.

Maisie was tempted by a tape of the *Muppet Movie*. She liked that one. It was on a sort of tape called a BetaMax, and it was only one penny, so it did seem a bargain, although she felt it might not work in their Blu-Ray DVD player. *No*, she thought, *I'll save my money for something special.*

She went methodically up and down the lines of tables, but everything that she could afford was smelly old junk. Junk she didn't feel like touching.

At last there was only one stall left. It was some way from the others under an oak tree and it was an interesting stall because it only had one thing left on it. An old lady sat in a tattered cane armchair behind the stall. She wore gloves with the fingers cut off, and a huge colourful scarf, which she wore like a shawl. Her gold earring made her look quite exotic, an image spoiled by her beret that had an army badge on it. She was talking to a girl with large sad eyes. The girl was about Maisie's age. As Maisie approached, they both turned and smiled.

'What's that?' asked Maisie, pointing to the thing on the table.

It was a bundle, wrapped in Christmas paper and sealed with yards of Sellotape wrapped round and round it. The bundle was clearly teddy-bear shaped.

'What's it look like, sweetie-pie?' smiled the old lady.

'It *looks* like a teddy bear,' said Maisie.

'Spot on.'

'Could I see it then?' asked Maisie.

'There it is, it's all gift-wrapped and ready to go,' said the old lady. 'It's quite old, but it looks brand new.'

'Why is it wrapped up?' asked Maisie.

'Well,' said the girl with sad eyes, speaking for the first time, 'it's an unwanted birthday present.'

'Why is a birthday present wrapped in paper with *Merry Christmas* on it, then?' said Maisie.

The sad eyes looked even sadder.

'It was a birthday present to somebody whose birthday was at Christmas!' interrupted the old lady quickly.

Maisie thought things out. Some quite old bears, even tatty old bears, were worth a lot of money on the *Roadshow*, especially those with a little metal button in their ear. Anyway, a girl can't have too many teddy bears.

'How much is it?' she asked.

'Ten pounds,' said the old lady.

'I've only got 10p,' said Maisie sadly.

The old lady and the girl with sad eyes looked at each other. 'That's near enough,' they said together.

When they all got home, Mum started to giggle as Dad tried on his Nikes. 'They make you look like a tramp!' she spluttered as he limped around the sitting room. 'They're like boats.'

'They'll be fine with three pairs of socks,' sniffed

Dad. 'And they don't smell as bad as your sandwich toaster!'

Maisie took her parcel up to her bedroom. She snipped the Sellotape with her nail scissors and tore off the paper. Surprisingly there was even more Sellotape inside, wrapped around the bear's head. She pulled it off carefully.

The teddy bear was wonderful. There was no little button in his ear, but he was in perfect condition. Both beady eyes were there, and he had no bald spots in his silky brown hair. Maisie bent his legs, and she sat him on her bed, on the pillow.

'I'll call you Ted,' she said.

Ted stared back. Maisie played happily all afternoon, pushing Ted this way and that, tucking him up and then dressing him in her clothes. Ted just stared.

'Maisie, are you ready for a sandwich?' It was Mum calling from downstairs.

'Please,' called Maisie. 'Can I have it up here?

'Sure,' said Mum. 'Would you like it toasted?'

Oh my God, thought Maisie, *she's trying out that toaster on me*. 'NO THANKS!' she called down quickly.

The sun was going down and her bedroom was washed with a strange light as Maisie finished her tuna mayonnaise sandwich, licked her fingers and picked up her glass of milk.

'Thank you *very* much!'

Maisie turned quickly, staring at Ted. She could not believe her ears. Ted stared back, and Maisie's heart quickened as the bear's beady eyes turned towards the empty plate.

'You spoke!' she croaked. The light in her bedroom became unreal. Ted sat in the gloom at the head of the bed, and Maisie gazed at him, her heart thumping.

'Yes,' said Ted. 'And you guzzled that entire sandwich. What about me? Don't I get anything to eat?'

'You can *speak*!'

'Course I can,' growled the bear. 'When I'm not starved to death, that is!'

'You can't eat as well?' said Maisie.

'Course I can, what d'you think these are for?' He opened his mouth, snapping small pointed teeth. 'Call your mum, and get some supper for me.'

'Don't be silly!' said Maisie.

'*Silly!*' roared Ted. 'I'll show you silly.' And he stood up.

Maisie backed away as Ted leaped to the floor and ran around the bedroom, throwing Maisie's books in the air and tearing out some of the pages. Then he jumped up and down until the room rattled.

'Maisie, stop that din!' shouted Dad from the bottom of the stairs. But Ted kept on jumping, so Dad came up the stairs and burst into the room. There were books all over the place and torn-out pages lying in heaps. 'What on *earth* have you done?' he gasped, looking around.

'I didn't do anything!' wailed Maisie. 'It was the bear.' She pointed to Ted, lying on his back amongst the litter, his legs in the air, his beady eyes staring at the ceiling.

'Maisie,' said Dad sharply, 'what have I always told you about fibbing? It gets you nowhere, especially stupid fibbing. Tidy your room, and let's have no more of it.' He slammed the door and stomped down the stairs.

Ted sat up and scowled. 'I'm *hungry*!' he insisted.

Maisie was getting angry now. She grabbed the bear, keeping clear of his snapping teeth. 'You'll get nothing till you behave yourself,' she hissed.

'We'll see about that!' snarled Ted, wriggling free. He ran over to a bedside table and, grabbing Maisie's alarm clock, he smashed it on the floor. Then he jumped onto the windowsill and danced along it, knocking a jam jar full of frogspawn and a china pony to the floor.

This time the noise brought Mum into the room. She stared at the smashed clock, at the china pony with no legs lying on the floor, and at the frogspawn soaking into the carpet, then she glared at Maisie.

'Dad told me what happened,' she said sharply.

'Maisie, I don't know *what* has come over you. Any more of this, and there will be *real* trouble.'

'It wasn't me!' wailed Maisie. 'It was that *bear*!' She pointed to Ted, now lying face down on the bed with his bum in the air.

Mum frowned at Maisie and stalked out of the room. She stopped at the door, turned round and said, 'I think it's about time you went to bed!'

Maisie didn't argue. She picked up Ted and stuffed him into her pants and vests drawer. 'Sleep tight!' she snapped, slamming the drawer shut.

Ted's reply was quite rude, for a teddy bear.

The next day, Maisie wore the same vest and pants – she didn't want to open that drawer! She gobbled down her breakfast and, for the first time in her life, she rushed to school.

When she got home from school, she went to her room and hauled Ted out of his drawer. He stretched and fixed Maisie with a beady eye.

'I'm *hungry*,' he growled.

Maisie folded her arms and poked Ted on the nose. 'Tell you what,' she said, 'I'll take you down to Mum and Dad, and you can tell them that I don't tell fibs.'

Ted glared. 'No way!' he snapped. 'I'm not a circus act. I don't perform in public.'

'Oh, don't you?' said Maisie. 'You'll get nothing to eat until you do.'

She grabbed Ted by one leg and thumped down the stairs. 'OUCH! OUCH! OUCH! OUCH!' squealed the bear, as his head bumped on every step.

Maisie got Mum and Dad onto the sitting-room sofa and sat Ted down facing them, in a comfy chair.

'Ladies and gentlemen,' she said, 'may I present Ted, the amazing talking bear.'

Mum looked blank and Dad glanced at his watch. Ted slumped over to one side.

'Say something,' hissed Maisie, hitting Ted on the head with a spoon.

Dad looked at his watch again, and Mum stood up. 'Ah, well, darling, that was nice, but now we've things to do,' she said, and together they wandered out of the sitting room.

Maisie grabbed Ted angrily round the neck and stomped upstairs. She slammed her bedroom door and glared at Ted.

'I'm HUNGRY!' moaned the bear, glaring back.

'Dream on!' snapped Maisie. 'Nothing, till you talk to Mum and Dad.'

The next evening Maisie tried again, with the same result. All Mum and Dad saw was a bog-ordinary teddy bear, and a daughter they were beginning to worry about. And after several more performances like that, they became quite concerned about their daughter. Maisie was also getting more and more angry, and Ted was getting very hungry indeed.

At last, the bear gave in. He was *so* hungry. 'All right, all right, all right,' he groaned, 'you win. I'll speak to 'em.'

The next day, Maisie settled her parents in the sitting room again and sat Ted down in his chair. She bowed towards her audience and introduced Ted.

All eyes were on the bear. There was a gasp when he stood up.

'Lady and gentleman,' he started, 'please understand this is not my idea, but I am to talk to you. Well, I don't know what to say to a man who looks like a tramp and a woman with no sense of smell.'

Everybody in the room sat up and Maisie stared.

'I suppose I could mention the time that you thought the bath had leaked so you called the plumber. Well, Maisie told me that was really her because she'd left the bath taps on.'

Maisie went white. 'Shut up!' she hissed.

'And the time that Maisie put cat food into your steak and kidney pie mix to see if Dad would notice.' Ted looked at Dad. 'And you didn't notice – in fact, you said it was delicious.'

Dad glared at Maisie. His mouth hung open. Maisie tried to hold Ted's nose shut.

'And that time,' said Ted struggling free, 'that time that Maisie cleaned the cat's teeth with Mum's toothbrush . . . and' – Maisie grabbed Ted and rushed to the door – 'the time Maisie put laxative chocolate in Gran's stocking, and Gran spent all Christmas in the bathroom, and' – Ted was shouting now as Maisie rushed into her bedroom – 'the time that Maisie put boot polish inside her uncle's shoes, and he went to see the doctor because his feet had turned black. And—'

Maisie managed to silence Ted by winding Sellotape round his snout, then bundling him up in brown paper. A muffled noise came from inside the paper, something about dead flies and Christmas pudding, until Maisie silenced Ted with layers of bubble wrap and a whole roll of Sellotape. She bundled the bear up so tightly he couldn't move.

Then she stuffed him back into her pants and socks drawer.

Next day, after school, her eighth best friend, Justin Slack, came round. Maisie left the bear-shaped parcel where he couldn't help seeing it.

'What's that?' he asked, pointing.

'Oh,' said Maisie, 'it's a valuable teddy bear, like the ones on the *Antiques Roadshow*.'

'Has it got a button in its ear?' asked Justin.

Maisie looked wise. 'No, it's far more unusual than that. I'm thinking of selling it to a rich American.'

'How much do you want for it?' asked Justin eagerly.

'Oh, I should think it's worth about a hundred pounds,' said Maisie carelessly.

'I'll give you twenty pence for it,' said Justin, his eyes shining.

'Fair enough,' said Maisie. 'It'll save me a trip to America!'

Quickly she handed the bear-shaped parcel to Justin and took his 20p.

A note about *Ted*

I've never owned a teddy bear (*ahhhhh!*). I never wanted one. So why now, when I am as grown up as anyone could possibly be, do I feel a sense of loss?

I suppose I always think of teddies as the perfect toy. More perfect than a computer, more lovable than a train set. Do you think that in years to come you will still have your old computer – or your old bear? My money is happily on the bear.

I also like car-boot sales. Well, I don't really, as I find them disappointing. I have never found treasure there; I've only ever bought things that the next day I wished I hadn't. So these two things came together in this story. A car-boot sale and the perfect toy . . .

Putting the record straight ...

Tony Ross was born in Wandsworth, South London, a year before the Second World War broke out. His family moved to Cheshire during the war to escape the Blitz. Here, he discovered a love of horses, and grew up desperate to become a jockey or a cowboy – at one point, he even wrote to the legendary actor John Wayne to ask if he could have a part in his next western! Tony's childhood was also a little bit theatrical – his father was a magician and his two uncles were actors.

Tony's other great passion was art, and as an only child, he spent long hours amusing himself by drawing. This love eventually took him to the Liverpool Regional College of Art, where he spent a lot of his time frequenting the Liverpool beat scene and listening to live music. Tony was also involved in local theatre and ballet productions and at one point, he even played the back legs of a pantomime cow!

When Tony left college, he went straight into advertising. But after a particularly bad day in his job as an art director, he left to teach design and typography, and started drawing cartoons for magazines including Punch.

This finally led Tony to writing and illustrating books. And he's been doing that ever since, with over 800 books to his name! His most famous series of picture books follows a wilful Little Princess, and the first title was published in 1986 with *I Want My Potty!* and there are now dozens of books following her adventures. Tony has also illustrated books by such authors as Michael Rosen, David Walliams, Jeanne Willis, Lynne Reid Banks and many more. He is particularly well known for his exuberant illustrations for Francesca Simon's *Horrid Henry* series.

It's not surprising that Tony has won plenty of acclaim for his books: *Dr Xargle's Book of Earth Tiggers* was shortlisted for the Kate Greenaway Medal and *Tadpole's Promise* won the Silver Medal in the Smarties Prize, *The Nanny Goat's Kid* was shortlisted for the Roald Dahl Funny Prize and *Hippospotamus* has been shortlisted for the Red House Children's Book Award.

Tony now lives on the Welsh border, and continues to work on plenty more children's books!

Choosing Crumble

By MICHAEL ROSEN
Illustrated by TONY ROSS

When Terri-Lee goes to the pet-shop, she thinks
she'll be choosing a dog – she doesn't expect the dog
to be choosing her! But Crumble is no ordinary pet
and he's got a few questions to ask:
How many walks will you take me on?
Do you like to dance?
Will you tickle me? I like that a lot.
Will Terri-Lee's dance moves and
answers be enough to convince
Crumble that she could be his
owner?

'Perfect for young readers'
The Bookseller

9781849395281 £4.99

The Not So Little Princess
COLOUR READER

What's My Name?

BY TONY ROSS AND WENDY FINNEY

The Little Princess is not so little any more!

Now that she's growing up, people can't keep calling her the LITTLE Princess. But her real name is horrible and no one dares tell her what it is!

What will the Not-so-Little Princess do when she finds out?

9781849395793 £4.99

The (Not So) Little Princess
COLOUR READER

Best Friends!

BY TONY ROSS AND WENDY FINNEY

Rosie has got a brand new friend!

Rosie's new friend
Ollie is different
in every way –
from his funny
old-fashioned way
of talking, to his
odd clothes.

And when they go
exploring, there's a
BIG surprise in store
for them . . .

9781849396301 £4.99

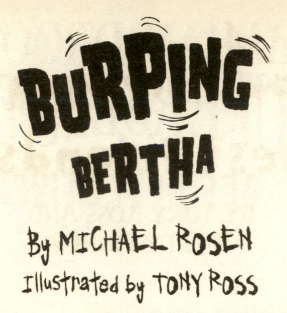

BURPING BERTHA

By MICHAEL ROSEN
Illustrated by TONY ROSS

On an ordinary morning, in an ordinary flat, an up–till–now perfectly ordinary Bertha does an extraordinary burp. A burp so extraordinary, it knocks things over. A burp so humongously big that very soon it's causing havoc in the school canteen, the playground, not to mention her grandad's apple trees ... Such a burptastic secret cannot stay quiet for long. And soon enough it lands Bertha her very own celebrity stardom ... but is it all just a lot of hot air?

'Harks back, like Horrid Henry, to the comic strips of Dennis the Menace or Minnie the Minx' *Telegraph*

9781849394062 £4.99

DAMIAN DROOTH
SUPERSLEUTH
ACE DETECTIVE

by Barbara Mitchelhill

with illustrations by
Tony Ross

Damian Drooth is a super sleuth, a number
one detective, a kid with a nose for trouble.
And here in this fantastic bumper edition are
three of his hilarious stories:

*The Case of the
Disappearing Daughter,
How to Be a Detective*
and *The Case of the
Popstar's Wedding.*

'Madcap cartoon-
sketch humour'
TES

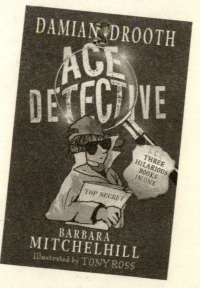

9781849390972 £5.99